BLOOD RED

SYRAH

In Vino Veritas

Steve Orbell

BLOOD RED SYRAH

A Gruesome California Wine Country Thriller

STEVE CORBETT

Design by Mat Giordano, Emily Rudolph and Kathryn Bondi
for Posture Interactive—Eye borrowed from Robyn's eye socket

Author photo by Clark Van Orden

To Stephanie, who, like me, is partial to pinot

FINISH YOUR WINE

L IFE's a beach. Then you die. California wine country's rich grape escape offers no guarantee of survival. Central Coastal chardonnay is killer in more ways than one.

But don't bother telling Wayne Wilson these fatal truths about the fruit of the vine. Wayne figured he'd live forever, drinking his winery's gold medal chard hard until the end of time. Fate at least granted this jackass half his wish; he died with a glass in his hand—and the cutting edge of pointed shards in his eye.

Chard, shard—you really need to know the difference. One can sometimes lead to the other. Wayne, though, refused to pay attention. That's why Wayne died sipping and slipping on his own fresh blood, tumbling like a drunken pageant queen into full wine barrels that crashed to the polished marble floor.

Mocking, taunting and laughing at his middle-aged, teary-eyed bastard son in the dank refuge of the chilled wine cave, that morning Wayne spit pure disdain—snobbishness as sour as the unripe grapes that grow for miles on swollen vines along both sides of the 101 freeway near Santa Barbara. Among Wayne's class of wine snob, a sneer is worth a thousand smiles.

"I gave you a job, you despicable failure. What more do you want?" Wayne said, staring deep into the golden chardonnay whirlpool he swirled in his glass.

Raising the goblet to his nose, Wayne closed his eyes and sniffed. Ah, creamy hints of freshly cut apple, persimmon, pear and cinnamon with a breath of suntan lotion. That's what made handcrafted Wilson chardonnay unique—always one weird scent, an olfactory scream that made Wayne's wine hip, the hippest wine on the Central Coast.

With this batch everybody, especially baby boomer tourists from New Jersey, swore they could detect Coppertone, Sea & Ski or Bain de Soleil even if they couldn't. Label deception is one of the wine industry's best kept secrets; nobody smells or tastes half the shit they say they smell and taste when they swirl a decanter under their nose and swear they detect berries.

"How about dingle berries? You smell them, too? Yes, you do. If I can smell that smell," smartass Wayne always said at the wine workshops and seminars he held around the world, "you can smell that smell."

"My brand is tailor-made to your tastes," Wayne said. "Even if you don't know what they are."

Everybody laughed at life-of-the-party Wayne even though they weren't sure what they were laughing at or why. For that crude condescension, local dilettantes and other suckers paid Wayne $68 a bottle—about $20 too much for even the best Cali chards.

As one of Santa Barbara County's pioneer wine merchants, Wayne did as he pleased. After opening one of the first boutique wineries in 1970, he trail-blazed, stayed the course, and benefitted from the industry's growing largesse and profitability.

"Finish your chardonnay," Wayne said to his estranged son. "We have nothing more to talk about. It's time for you to leave."

A shy man in clean white Pumas he scrubbed with Ajax, Wally wore fresh white socks, pressed blue slacks from Sears and a lime green polo shirt with a palm tree emblem on the pocket. Soft at 44, balding and an acute embarrassment to his hapless Generation X, Wally wanted to cry.

"You acted like I wasn't even alive," he said in almost a whisper to his father. "You never acknowledged my existence."

"We have nothing in common except your mother," Wayne said. "I paid her all these years to keep you from pestering me. I grudgingly gave you the job as a tasting room attendant as a favor to finally buy her out. Favor for a failure. Favor for two failures."

"Mommy is very sick."

"Mommy is sick all right. From guzzling the Two-Buck Chuck she buys at Trader Joe's and anything else she could find over the years. And when the wine ran out? Jesus Christ. Did she ever mention her Ice Blue Aqua Velva cocktail when she hit bottom last year? You ever wonder what happened to your aftershave lotion? She called me and I hung up on her. Your mother is worse than sick. "

Actually, Wally was drinking too much, too, worrying he was becoming an alcoholic, adding to his anxiety, his odd mood swings, his depression and fear.

"She wants me to tell you she forgives you," Wally said.

"Ha," Wayne said.

Laughing out loud, he poured himself another glass of wine.

"Did she ever mean anything to you?" Wally asked.

"Mary Jane was 21 and hot, nothing more than another food paring on a sweltering summer night in the vineyard. A skinny asparagus stalk teamed with a full-bodied chardonnay. That's about it. A few weeks of tasting and I was ready for the next course."

Using his pinkie, Wayne wiped a splash of wine from both sides of his thick blond moustache, which, along with golden Liberace-like hair, a stylist in Montecito dyed boisterous custard yellow every week to match the buttery hues of his award-winning chardonnay. Other than dyed hair, Wayne stayed relatively authentic, fit at 70, with regular massage, tennis, golf and hikes he took to hassle and sexually harass the help in the vineyards.

"Pouring world-class chardonnay in my tasting room in Los Olivos was good enough for her until she got cute and got pregnant," Wayne said. "Serving tourists should have been good enough for you. But, as I can see, and it pains me to say what I see, you are not equipped with social skills or marketable talent of any kind. You still don't even know how to properly hold your stemware."

Looking at the wine glass, the globe of which he cupped inexpertly in his hand, Wally fumbled to change his grip. Now holding tightly to the stem with two fingers balancing the base, Wally worried he might drop the expensive crystal. Carefully raising the glass, he inserted his nose and sniffed, sensing notes of vanilla, pepper and passion fruit swirling in his head with a growing touch of madness and a wild bouquet of murder.

"Ready for the finish, Wally?" asked the voice in his head that about a month earlier had politely introduced herself as "Syrah" and said she was a friend and lifetime spiritual guide.

Wally remembered the community college wine education course he took before going to work at the winery. The last impression of a wine is called the finish. Wally wanted the sharp voice to go away but, for some reason, he liked and trusted Syrah. Without thinking, he knew she was right when she said, "Your last impression of Daddy-O here is called the big finish."

"Is this better, Father?" Wally said, smiling now, raising the glass just so, as if looking at a rainbow through the sparkling clean surface of the expensive goblet.

Anger overwhelmed the wine master.

"You dare call me Father? Father? Why you little loser. Don't you ever call me ...."

Moving with the darting ease of a ruby-throated humming-bird zig-zagging in and out of the tan branches of an avocado tree, Wally swung the glassware, catching Wayne at the hairline above his right eyebrow. The force of the blow and the first piece of breaking glass cut deeply into thin skin, drenching him in perfectly chilled chardonnay and quickly exposing white bone before rich red blood began to flow.

Not knowing what hit him, Wayne froze.

With the aplomb of a tuxedoed orchestra conductor thrusting the baton at a Santa Barbara Bowl symphony concert, Wally twisted the glass stem, shoving the sharp edge deeper into his father's face, splitting the already open incision with the ease of a jeweled letter opener slicing into a business envelope. For good measure, Wally twisted the stem again, even deeper.

Classic instrumental surf music erupted in Wally's head, like a vintage jukebox blasting off all by itself on a warm night in 1961 at the Rendezvous Ballroom on Balboa Beach. Fender guitar and bongos pounded an electric jungle beat deep into his brain stem, sending bad vibrations sparking down his spine and into the raw nerve endings of his body.

Like Dick Dale and his Del-Tones, Wally was tripping. Syrah dancing the Watusi in his head made him wackier. With her shaking and going to a-go-go, Wally imagined her stuffed into a wild fringed bikini like a hundred bunnies in a beach blanket movie from more innocent times when Frankie and Annette seemed to really love each other. Times changed and not for the better.

A shining 24 karat gold corkscrew on the bar caught Wally's eye—an inscribed commemorative award the Santa Barbara Vintner's Association presented Wayne on the occasion of his first world championship batch of what the connoisseurs called "burnt straw" chardonnay.

Riveted now with bloodlust, Wally grabbed and opened the utensil. Bending at the waist and hooking like a desperate middleweight boxing champion, he plunged the long metal spiral deep into his father's right eye, turning the screw clockwise with the expertise of a beachside sommelier. The 5-turn worm bit deep inside the fibrous tunic of Wayne's eyeball, tightly gripping the cornea. Turning the screw again, Wally dug into the middle layer uvea, gouging into the clear gel vitreous. Reaching with his left hand, Wally grabbed a fist full of Wayne's silky lemon hair that smelled strangely of suntan lotion and felt delicate, soft as egg yolk-colored poppies growing free on a barren mesa.

Wally started to pull. Soft and mushy, the eyeball oozed rather than popped. Disappointed, Wally wanted the eye to burst from the socket with the exploding sound of a sparkling wine cork on New Year's Eve. Instead, a small sigh of extraction hissed from the cavity like a dying rattlesnake. Wayne fainted and fell to the cold floor.

"Outta sight, Wally," said Syrah. "Outta sight."

Wally dropped the corkscrew with whatever eyeball detritus was still attached.

"Screw you, Dad," he said.

Blood overflows a decanter as easily as pinot noir or chardonnay. Central Coastal wine country isn't always peacefully intoxicating—sophisticated or eye-popping, if you will—with aromas of ginger, Spanish moss and saddle leather. Sometimes the nose gets broken. Sometimes people die. Texture isn't everything.

Don't expect wealthy vintners who make money from oenology to tell you to expect trouble as you taste. Still, you better beware as you travel from Montecito through Goleta and past the soft Irish green hills of the Santa Maria Valley. Danger smells of pomegranate privilege, coconut cream customs and seasoned wine greed from the silent Santa Barbara mansions owned by bloated plutocrats, through gritty Santa Maria farmworker housing, north to liberal academic San Luis Obispo, and on to San Francisco and beyond where the wild weed grows.

As we begin our deadly journey, a wandering wine trail awaits Wally who has already started his personal harvest.

QUEEN OF THE HIPPIES

FUNERAL services for Mary Jane Zook—born April 1, 1951, died October 8, 2017—lasted ten minutes. Laid out in her most colorful sundress decorated with yellow sunflowers and purple daisies—new Birkenstock sandals, too—she seemed peaceful and asleep when the funeral director closed the lid and wheeled the cardboard casket off to meet the flames of cremation.

Wally wept, softly touching the quarter-sized sterling silver peace sign his mother wore around her neck every day since she bought the cherished trinket in Haight-Asbury during the Summer of Love in '67.

Mary Jane had just turned sixteen when she hit Golden Gate Park for the Grateful Dead concert—a "happening" as she called it when she told Wally the story dozens of times before he went to bed as a tyke—mommy's little flower child, she called him.

Now Wally wore the necklace and bemoaned the passing of the gentle West Coast goddess who taught him all he knew about life—and now death.

Mary Jane, named after a sweet treat by her mother who loved the peanut butter and molasses taffy-type candy, named her only child after a television show.

Wally, played by Tony Dow, was the oldest son on "Leave It to Beaver," the iconic baby boomer television show that presented the American family in ways most families did not live in America. Wayne Wilson told Mary Jane that first night in the vineyard that Wally Cleaver was the kind of all-American boy after whom he had modeled his own life as a kid growing up in Montecito surrounded by other privileged sons of wealthy capitalists and in later years, of course, Oprah. Just as June, Ward and the Beav knew their Wally was perfect, Wayne's parents knew he was even better.

Mary Jane told the nurse before they wheeled her out of the delivery room that night in 1973 that her little Wally was better than perfect. To her he was manna from heaven. Maybe his name would bring Wayne to her side, with flowers, a nice bottle of wine, a ring and, yes, as she allowed herself to dream, a marriage proposal.

After supper and orange Jell-O that night in the hospital, a security guard showed up at her bedside.

"This is for you," he said.

Inside the manila tan envelope Mary Jane found a contract, all spelled out in legalese and awaiting her signature. The small cottage-style house would be in her name and belong to her as long as she abided by the stipulations that followed: No contact with Wayne or members of his family. No trespassing on winery property. No mention of his role in her pregnancy for as long as she lived and, above all, no surprises. Wayne led an orderly life that could not under any circumstances be complicated by truth that did not coincide with his view of the world and his place in it.

Mary Jane signed the deal within an hour.

On her way out of the hospital the next day, she mailed the contract to the post office box address on the return envelope, kissed Wally and told him she would be the best mommy in the whole wide world.

"Let's go home to our new house," Mary Jane said.

Located on a quiet side street not far from downtown Santa Barbara and the hustle of State Street, the house, built in 1945, was lovely. The lawn was small but manicured nicely. An avocado tree stood tall and full in the front yard. Mary Jane thought the house was beautiful, far nicer than the rented one-story red brick where Mary Jane grew up in Duncannon, Pennsylvania, before she ran away to join the hippies.

Within a week Mary Jane had decorated the nursery with balloons, painting the walls with characters she knew Wally would like from television cartoons, comic books and nursery rhymes when she was in elementary school. Bunnies and dancing flowers joined doe-eyed fawns and friendly ladybugs, looking down from the ceiling and the walls on this fine new child.

In her room, until she could buy a mattress for the floor, she laid out the sleeping bag she bought at the Army Navy Store for her hitchhiking trip across the country. Incense and drippy wax candles in wine bottles made her feel like she was queen of the hippies. Mary Jane owned a transistor radio, three pair of blue jeans and some nice silk print blouses. Mostly she went barefoot. Unemployed since her pregnancy, she only wore flip flops to the supermarket. The expense check from Wayne arrived promptly every month, more than enough for her and Wally to get by. After the insult and threats from Wayne's lawyers, Mary Jane felt free.

The house became their happy home. No men allowed, though. Mary Jane never brought a man home. When she meditated in the yoga room she designed with bamboo stalks stuck in sky blue Mexican vases, cheap tatami mats and fluffy printed pillows, she sat quietly doing nothing, just waiting for Wayne—Wayne, his name her mantra, her inspiration, her vision that one day would lead to her enlightenment. Wally would one day have his daddy and together they would go to the beach, eat fish tacos and laugh in the sun—a family for everyone to see, so very happy together. But, other than Wally's true love, none of Mary Jane's dreams ever came true.

"Promise me you won't cry at my funeral," she said to Wally the morning she died.

"Mommy, don't," Wally said.

"I have a new pair of sandals in my closet. But I'm out of Two-Buck Chuck. You should buy some cases for the wake. An Irish wake. Have a nice little Irish wake for your mother."

Wally's sadness caught in his throat, choking his response as he tightly shut his eyes against the tears.

"Above all, tell Wayne Wilson I never told a soul about you, Wally, about you being his son."

Feeling a horrible wave of nausea, Wally stiffened. Pangs of sorrow went head-to-head with ribald confusion, blending with excitement that battled despair. Physical shudders went to his head, causing brain freeze ten times worse than a summertime ice cream headache, attacking his deepest feelings with barbed paranoia. Anxiety shot through his nervous system like a laser laxative through his colon. He got dizzy. The room swirled like the bad acid trips his mother sometimes talked about in her sleep. Wally thought he might collapse, go into shock, or take a fit.

"I'm Wayne Wilson's son?" he said. "Wayne Wilson is my father?"

"Yes," she said. "Tell your daddy I forgive him. Tell him I'm sorry I wasn't what I should have been for him. Tell him our little house is worth a fortune now and that I'm grateful for all he did for us."

Syrah spoke.

"Tell daddy to go fuck himself, too," she said.

Wally tried not to let on that a shrill voice just screamed in his head and that maybe his mother heard the insult.

"So I'm not Jim Morrison's love child like you told me," Wally said.

"No, honey" Mary Jane said.

"And Jerry Garcia didn't buy you this house and set you up for life after you convinced him at Woodstock that you were the Blessed Mother?"

"Sorry."

"I never believed any of that, anyway."

"I wanted what was best for you."

"That's why I grew up to be a nut?"

"You are not a nut."

"I am nuts."

"You have some emotional issues, baby, but you're just fine. A little eccentric, maybe, but otherwise you're my groovy little boy."

"Don't let your mother sweet talk you, Wally," said Syrah. "Don't let her bullshit you. You are absolutely nuts."

Wally gasped, snapping out of the familial freak-out. Quickly looking behind him he worried that a stranger had entered the house, a drunk or a deranged mental patient. But no one was there. Sometimes he forgot Syrah lived in his head. Syrah was becoming bolder, though, telling Wally her aggression was for his own good.

Syrah even offered to speak for him whenever he got tongue-tied.

"You go now, Wally," Mary Jane said. "Go to the winery. Tell your father I told you who you are. Tell him to be the man I always hoped he'd be."

"I don't want to see him," Wally said. "Don't make me go."

"Please, Wally. Do it for me. Do it for your dear old hippie mother."

Mary Jane forced a smile, reached for her radio and turned on the classic rock station. She grabbed a handful of Mary Janes from a chipped candy dish on the end table and knocked over her half-empty wine glass.

Wally bit his lower lip to keep from crying once again, turned and opened the door.

"Wait for me, dude," Syrah said. "This is one happy hour at the winery I don't want to miss."

Setting off on this memorable day in paradise, Wally and his audibly gleeful imaginary companion entered deeper into the chaos than he—or she—had ever ventured. Slipping away forever from his mother's love, sinking into the gross turmoil of a madman run amok through the quicksand of his worst dysfunction, for the first time in his life Wally was on his own.

"Don't forget me, fucker," Syrah said.

FAR OUT

After paying all the bills and taking care of Mary Jane's few matters of unfinished business—her meager will with contributions to the soup kitchen, the women's center and the ACLU—Wally donated his much used but well-cared for Subaru to a local nonprofit environmental group dedicated to saving from extinction the Snowy Plover, the dainty dune bird that local Republicans called the other white meat.

Then Wally walked away from the house sale with $714,000 in his checking account that never before held more than a few hundred dollars at a time, $30,000 of which he used to buy an almost mint condition 1966 Volkswagen camper painted like a psychedelic rainbow that he saw advertised in the Santa Barbara Independent by a former roadie for Crosby, Stills, Nash & Young who lived near Crosby in Santa Ynez.

"Kept the bus in the garage and forgot all about it," the roadie said.

Wally laughed for the first time since his mother died. Still nervous because Santa Ynez was as far away from home as Wally had ever travelled, he tried to relax and enjoy the moment.

"I worry she won't ever get out on the road again," the roadie said. "I worry she's finished."

"That's not nice," Wally said, suddenly feeling dizzy, light-headed and afraid. "It's nice to be nice."

"You got that right, man," the roadie said. Patting the side of the van, he said, "Where would you like to take her?"

"Haight-Ashbury," Wally said. "Golden Gate Park. Looking for a love-in."

Laughing hard, the roadie reached into the pocket of a red and black beaded and fringed leather jacket. Pulling out a fat rolled joint he said, "Take this for the trip, partner."

Stamping the ground in a little dance, the roadie kicked up dust with black leather cowboy boots with snakeskin tips. Rocking back on his heels he looked skyward, as billowy white clouds in the shape of musical notes rolled by.

"Sure wish I was going with you, brah. But those days are gone," he said.

"Not for me they're not," Wally said. "Brah."

Now both men laughed, brothers of the universe getting by in the psycho void of a mad 21st century bound to get worse. Wally never felt this good. After eavesdropping on surfers and freaks and homeless people talking on State Street for years, calling each other "brah" like East Coast hipsters called each other "bro," Wally had never called anybody "brah" in his life. Now he was with it. Now he was cool. Wally felt groovy.

After leaving everything behind, Wally wanted desperately to see and feel and hear what his mother saw and heard and felt when she was most alive—San Francisco and the Jefferson Airplane and getting high and Stinson Beach in the summertime. But the Airplane was gone and getting high scared Wally, who had never smoked a joint. Drinking was bad enough and was getting worse, with monster hangovers in the morning and its unpredictable tenor, especially recently, when temper, rather than a simple, mellow drunk seemed to overwhelm him with the power of a rogue wave crashing a tent at El Capitan Beach.

Wally took the joint and thanked his benefactor.

"Are you like a guru?" he asked.

"Yeah, my abracadabra word is 'beyond,'" the roadie said.

"Thank you, man," Wally said. "I want to go beyond, too."

Wally handed over the cash.

The VW bus engine turned over as smoothly as sand from an hour glass marking the next second in a joyous lifetime. Easily moving the gear shift into first, Wally gently let out the clutch,

giving "her" some gas as he eased onto the highway and into traffic. Hitchhiking, just like his mother had done in her youth, had
taken Wally four hours to get to the roadie's house in the canyon off
Route 154 on the San Marcos Pass road. But he enjoyed every second. With money in the bank and cash in his canvas knapsack, as
well as about a dozen cheap corkscrews he had picked up for some
unknown reason at a hardware store before leaving Santa Barbara,
Wally felt like an intrepid traveler on his way to the first real good
adventure of his new life.

After finally parting company with the past, with his peace
sign and love beads necklace, he wore a new blue denim shirt with
snap pearl buttons, new blue jeans and new black Arizona-style
Birkenstocks. Vowing never to cut his hair until the ends reached
his waist, Wally ran his hand over a creeping bald spot and absolutely felt hippie hair growing there already. In a leather wallet his
mom made him for his 40th birthday, he carried a driver's license, a
bank ATM card and $5,000 in bills.

"Right on," Wally yelled out the open window. "Right on."

Syrah screamed.

"Up against the wall, motherfucker," she said.

JESUS JUICE

WHAT must it have been like when Michael Jackson opened the Neverland gates and all the laughing children rushed in? How thrilled they must have been, running from one free all-you-can-eat ice cream stand to the next, riding the merry-go-round with the calliope music playing and the carved painted horses going up and down and up and down and so much fun you never wanted to get off the ride.

Wally stood outside the gates to an empty, desolate Neverland, closed, vacant and for sale, its guard shack unoccupied and no uniformed security checking the IDs of countless celebrities who once flowed through those gates like Jesus juice, the name the child victim testified Michael called the wine he gave him and his brother to drink.

Chilled wine is one thing; child wine is poison, Wally thought.

Children, mostly poor kids Michael groomed for what he called friendship and love, were the focus of a never-ending-land of perversion. Wally believed the little boy's story, the child who testified that the grooming was molestation, touching, violating and sexual abuse.

Wally followed news of the sordid case closely. No matter what the jury decided, he knew Michael was guilty. The sick stories made Wally's heart hurt. Mary Jane said she pitied Michael but wanted jurors to convict him based on solid evidence she believed. Cops, prosecutors and district attorney staff put together a sound case. However else they acted like macho boors, they had done their jobs. Jurors and most of the press hated the alleged victim's Latina mother, raised on hard streets in East Los Angeles, trying to do what was best for her children even if she put her trust in the wrong person.

Feeling sorry for her, Wally believed her story, too.

One day Wally thought about driving the hour to Santa Maria for the 2005 trial to stand outside the courthouse by the wire security fence with Michael's hysterical fans from all over the world to see how he felt, to find out if he could do anything to help the children Michael and people like Michael hurt. Fear overcame Wally's best instincts, though, and he stayed home, watching the TV news and reading trial coverage in the local newspapers. The Santa Maria Mirror news columnist covering the trial knew Michael was guilty, too, and told the story as it unfolded each day in court. Wally liked that truth mattered to him. Truth should matter to everybody.

Now here stood Wally at the scene of the crime. The massive estate sprawled on the other side of winding hills that led from the gate. Wally could see nothing from the bygone days of endless dirty secrets and terror disguised as innocence. No little choo-choo train, no private movie theater equipped with glass cases filled with endless rows of free candy bars for little hands to grab, not even the dirty disheveled flamingos Michael eventually ignored just like he ignored the deterioration of his mind.

If Michael's mind could go bad, what hope did Wally have?

Headlights coming his way shined on the other side of a hill. A gold Rolls Royce followed a new red BMW. Both cars stopped at the gate. Nobody in either car had yet seen Wally standing in the shadows.

Then they did.

As the gate swung open, blond real estate broker Amber Black's outrage simply could not be contained.

"Can I help you?" she said.

Wally got scared but was too afraid to run.

"I'm just looking," he said.

A man wearing a tight black t-shirt, a white linin suit and raspberry suede loafers with no socks stepped from the Rolls. Wally stared at his spiky gelled hair that made him look like a cartoon porcupine. Even in small circles of California wealth, the man was too old for this kind of styling but must have thought his appearance did him some good in whatever line of work he was in—which, as it turned out, was German pornography set to martial marching music.

Dieter Stone, tan, sloppy and lecherous, liked to say he could match a client to every fetish. More German marching porn addicts existed in Central Coastal California than anywhere in the world, he said. And, believe it or not, they were everywhere.

"Well, well, well," Stone said. "Look at this. The last of the Michael Jackson fans."

"No sir," Wally said. "I'm not a fan. I just stopped to look."

Countless people over the years made the pilgrimage to Los Olivos and took the turn at Figueroa Mountain Road, driving another five miles or so just to look at the entrance to the most notorious piece of property this side of O.J.'s house on Rockingham.

"You were going to graffiti a message on one of the stones in the wall, weren't you?" Stone said. "You were going to vandalize this property and decrease its value, weren't you? Write something like 'I love you more?' Maybe you're a pervert, too. Like Michael. Is that what you are, another freaky Michael Jackson weirdo?"

Surf music and bongos ignited in Wally's head. Syrah prepared to dance her favorite Watusi.

"I am so sorry, Dieter," Amber Black said. "Follow me to the café and I'll buy you a bottle of their best chardonnay to seal the deal. You've made the right decision to buy the ranch. In a year the Russians or the Chinese will be willing to pay you double for the place."

"Yes, they will, Fraulein," Stone said.

By the time they returned their attention to Wally, he had slipped into the darkness, walking toward the private school down the road where he had parked the van.

Two hours later, when Dieter's Rolls pulled away from the café, Wally followed at a discreet distance.

Surf guitar got louder.

Wally heard big bongos.

HERE KITTY, KITTY

California roadside diners create a greasy aura all their own, a down-and-out burnt bacon luster of blistering cooking oil, hot sauce and unwashed dishes that smell spent, like stale Pall Mall ashes collecting in an abandoned beer can that months ago rolled under the stove. Not nearly good enough for trendy beautiful people, these lard bowls draw outlaw bikers like dung beetles to a rodeo horse corral.

Members of the Crushers Motorcycle Club gathered daily at Dope's Diner.

Owner and ex-convict Dope Ventura, who hailed from Ventura and swore on a stack of lies that his family founded the city, made a name for himself at the California Men's Colony near San Luis Obispo where he worked as a cook and ladled out fried cockroaches in a thick spicy sautéed tomato sauce for VIP corrections officers who organized an illegal pop-up prison kitchen/cafeteria for prison staff and believed they were getting free gourmet fusion food from a seasoned Southern California restaurant chef doing time on methamphetamine charges.

"Don't tell me. Crunchy jalapenos with soy stuffing, right?"

"Man, how did you know?"

When a captain and two lieutenants fell ill and Dope's culinary skills came under suspicion, he quickly loaded up a tomato roach bowl peppered with real jalapenos and garlic, gobbled the entre, belched and asked who else was hungry for his crunchy specialty. The hacks lined up with Styrofoam take-out containers to bring home leftovers for the wife and kids.

Starting out as a dare before turning up on the menu, badass bikers at Dope's sucked down the vermin specialty with lime and hot sauce. Prospects in the club ate their roaches without condiments. Consciously eating sautéed roaches—hot sauce or no hot sauce—takes a special kind of degenerate. Dope's was loaded with lowlifes.

"I'm not serving this shit to anybody anymore," Rose said. "There's something wrong with you, Dope, to knowingly serve big bugs to these biker mongrel savages."

"At Dope's, the customer is always right," Dope said. "Crunchy cucarachas is and will remain the Wednesday night all-you-can-eat '1 percenter special' until further notice."

"These maniacs are eating cockroaches like they're barbecued fava beans," Rose said.

"At five dollars a head," Dope said. "And I never run out of product. Just go to the walk-in refrigerator and flip on the light. Dope's never skimps on protein."

Rose sensed a bizarre streak of pride in his voice.

"Just trying to outdo each other with what gross righteous bikers they are," Rose said.

"Yeah, but Animal's different—he was trying to impress you."

"By eating cockroaches."

"You don't get to wear Crushers colors unless you go all the way. You ever notice that Animal eats more than anybody. Man wants you to notice."

"You saw what he did last night," Rose said. "Animal tried to kiss me after eating a bowl full of bugs. I should have shot him."

"You're not still carrying a gun to work?"

Rose didn't answer.

"You were right to let me handle it," Dope said. "But what you did was worse. You embarrassed him in front of his people, called him out in front of his brothers. You told him he was a primitive species all by himself, that he was worse than a cockroach alive or dead. Animal took the abuse because he likes you. That's why he walked out without saying a word or taking my place apart. But he'll be back. Oh, yeah, he'll be back."

"I'm quitting next week," Rose said. "You used to run a nice place. I'd rather go back to dancing."

"I go to trial next week on fentanyl charges." Dope said. "I needed to make fast money and lots of it however I could for my lawyer. Crispy critters were a stroke of genius."

With that the door opened and in walked Animal, smelling of the strong soap he used to wash his nest of hair for the first time in a week. Thirty years old, at six-foot-four, 236 pounds, with blacktop hair falling to the middle of his back. Primal DNA flowed through his body with the force of fresh steroids, creating a thick primeval beard and moustache that matched his black eyebrow—one connected streak of unevolved hair from temple to temple, as unruly as a possum caught in a barbed wire penitentiary fence.

Beneath a stained, cracked leather vest, Animal's shoulders rippled with muscles he developed from lifting homemade barbells—coffee cans filled with cement connected by a rough iron bar he stole from a construction site. On his arms, red, blue and green tattoos of broken skulls, howling demons and screaming open-mouthed nymphs surrounded by flames shined beneath overhead diner lights that slow danced with the lost colors of hell.

Wallace Anderson, 28 and wiry, saw him coming and immediately stood from his seat near the revolving pie display. As president of the Crushers, he controlled all outbursts. But he hadn't seen Animal to talk with him since Animal punched the diner's screen door off the hinges, kicked over the Harley-Davidson Panhead engine, and tore into the night. Wallace left a note on the door to Animal's room at the motel where he lived and worked as a handyman. Saying he'd rather surprise people than call them, Animal refused to own a phone. Animal was full of surprises.

Dope and Rose tried to stay calm.

Taking a seat on a counter stool at the end of the diner, Animal hunched over his paper placemat full of trivia facts about West Coast surfing. Whispering to himself, cradling something inside his half-zipped vest, he made mini kissing sounds. Nobody spoke at the booths and tables.

"I'm telling him to leave," Rose said.

"Not a good idea," Dope said.

Making a slow walk down the counter past a petrified customer who pushed back, swiveled on his stool and stepped away from his plate of beans and meatloaf, Rose felt anger gather in her belly. Nobody in her twenty-nine years had ever tried to kiss her without permission—whether they just ate insects or not. Nobody disrespected her without her doing something about it.

As she neared Animal, the Crushers' sergeant at arms, club goon and no-two-ways-about-it-muscle, Rose sensed something soft, something small, something furry nestled just inside his jacket. Slowing her walk in the most comfortable old-fashioned white waitress shoes she owned, Rose hesitated and stopped. Animal didn't seem to notice as she wiped her hands on her apron and leaned in to listen.

"Good kitty," he whispered into his armpit. "You're my good little kitty cat."

Now Rose whispered.

"Oh my God," she said.

Just visible inside Animal's vest, the brown and white fur on top of a tiny kitten's head gently blew in the cool breeze of the overhead fan. Animal's right forefinger, on which he wore a Satan's head ring with tiny red glass eyes, left a downy indentation in the fur as he traced a path in the kitten's coat.

Looking up, Animal gave Rose a look she could only decipher as shy.

"I was out of line last night," he said. "I was so wrong. Will you forgive me?"

Rose stood speechless.

"And, when you're not busy, will you please bring me a saucer of warm milk for my kitty."

Staring with her hand covering her mouth, Rose's eyes began to tear.

"Of course," she said. "Of course I will and I will."

Wallace looked at the fake pressed tin ceiling and wanted to close his eyes—keep them closed for a very long time. Sleep, maybe forever. This Animal act was unique all right, brand new, but he had seen the man in action before. Never like this, though. The club thug had sure put some thought into this one. No good had ever come from Animal's planned drama in the past. No good would come from this one. In a pinch Animal always made life go from bad to worse, especially when he figured he had nothing to lose— which was almost always. This one might be the worst premeditation of them all. Wallace gave the scene his undivided attention and got ready for the worst.

Nobody moved or spoke until Rose came back with the saucer of milk she had warmed on the lowest flame on the diner gas stove. Walking gingerly so as not to spill a drop, she gently placed the saucer in front of Animal. Looking up at Rose, he winked one emerald green eye and took a deep chest-expanding breath that lightly nudged the kitten's delicate ears that hung like floppy flower petals over the feline's face.

Then Rose came face-to-face with insanity.

In a flash Animal pulled the severed kitten's head from inside his vest and shook it to the heavens. Slamming the eyes-open gore into the saucer of milk, the dish crashed to the floor, shattering as the mangled cat head rolled on the stained linoleum until it stopped nose up, its little ears soaked in a pink soup of skim milk and fresh gristle.

Animal looked directly at Rose and snarled.

"Here kitty, kitty, kitty," he said.

Moving toward his prey, he tried to cut her escape from behind the counter.

But mid-grab his words cut out; his eyes locked in place like the steel opening through which the prison guards used to slide him his dinner slop when he was in solitary, serving time in the hole for bad conduct. Violent muscle contractions spun Animal 180 degrees, felling him like a human redwood convulsed in a grand mal seizure. Nine Crushers held him down, keeping him there as he twitched and they looked to Wallace to tell them what to do next.

Rose had cleared the counter in one leap and sprinted into the parking lot. Wallace stood over Animal, seeing nothing but raw evil in his catatonic expression. The brute did not speak. Wallace turned and walked away without a word.

"C'mon, Prez," one Crusher said. "What the fuck, man?"

By this time two customers discreetly called 911 from the men's room. A teenage dishwasher under the influence of bath salts caught the whole scene on cellphone video and had already posted to Facebook and YouTube. Dope worried about the cops and the Crushers.

Wallace kept going.

Rose passed by when Wallace pulled his bike to the shoulder of the freeway after seeing her walking alone about a mile up the road.

"Want a ride?" he said.

Rose climbed on the scooter and held tightly to Wallace's chest as they pitched forward together, racing into the unknown feeling more than a little dead inside. Both quiet, they rode nonstop for hours into another day and another place, hopefully one where the unknown might not be so cruel and sad for kitty cats and other living things.

JUST DISAPPEAR

Twenty years earlier, in a part of Los Angeles called El Monte, a serious woman with swollen ankles in an orchid-colored skirt adjusted her blue and red shawl-like rebozo over a soft white blouse decorated with green shells and a few pieces of delicate white lace.

Distracted, despite her love of cooking, she thought of her son, Jesús.

Even a Mexican witch must prepare for heartbreak.

Stirring a deep copper pot full of mole sauce with a spoon twice as big as a piñata bat, Zita smelled the sweet/hot aroma of chocolate and red pepper. Today marked her son's 25th birthday, a time of great celebration and optimism. After the party tonight at Taco Ranchero, she would let him go, just disappear as her three spiritual guides told her she must. No traces, they said, just go. Jesús must find his path, come to grips with the ancestry and animal nature he possesses—the essence that possesses him—and grow into the image of Jesús Malverde from whom he descended. Then he will find you and come home, the guides said.

"What about the legacy of his blood?" Zita said. "When will I tell him his real identity?"

"No one speaks of this lineage," said the first guide. "No one talks of his bloodline."

"Three men dead, all hanged," Zita said. "Jesús, his great-grandfather, Jesús, his grandfather and Jesús, his father—all cursed by the rich. All condemned to die for the people."

"Your son must not know until he is able to carry the burden," said the second guiding voice. "Assuming he is able to carry the burden."

"He will rise," Zita said.

"The danger will rise as well," said the third spiritual guide. 'The danger will follow him."

"How long until he appears in Culiacan? In Sinaloa? In Mexico?" Zita said.

"As long as it takes."

"I will return to Culiacan tomorrow."

"A long time has passed since you walked those dusty streets. You have never visited the chapel, never prayed at the shrine."

"Once I return I will go every day."

"And then one day your son will come."

"And we will go to the shrine together," Zita said. "My Jesús will rid the streets of the evil. He will cleanse the bullet casings from the gutters forever and protect good people who need his help. My son will avenge the deaths of the Malverde family."

"Enjoy his party tonight. Then let him go."

Bubbling mole sent a deep candied aroma through the small house in East LA. Norteño music blasted from down the street where cholos waiting to score hung on the corner. Flaco the skinny Chihuahua yipped at her feet, demanding attention and a treat. Zita threw him a wrinkled cooked chicken foot she used to season the bitter brown sauce and watched Flaco attack.

Jesús never expressed interest in his father or his father's side of the family. Maybe out of respect, maybe out of fear, Zita was not sure. But now he wanted to know, said he needed to know, yearned to understand his past. Now he was asking questions she had done her best to avoid.

Past mattered.

As for her, she was who she was, a "bruja," or witch, from Oaxaca who one day left her dusty village and took the bus to Culiacan to find a better life. The day she arrived, a gentle, rugged man protected her from clumsy men wearing new boots and hand-stitched suits who mocked her language and long braided black hair and made her weep into her hands.

After helping her find a room and a kitchen job at a restaurant, the man respectfully returned each week to check on her safety. No one ever laughed at her again. One year after her arrival, he asked if she would marry him. Of course she said she would. Of course she did.

Just one week into the marriage, corrupt local police came for her husband, hung him from a tree in the park square, and left his body to rot as an example of what happens when you challenge ill-bred men who own the system. Three days later, federal police cut him down. By that time Zita was gone on a bus to the border frontier where, after becoming separated from her group and lost in the desert, she made her way across the border. Guided by a mysterious silver coyote—a four-legged animal, not a two-legged bandit—she slipped unannounced into the United States and a promise of freedom. About nine months later she gave birth to baby Jesús and gave him her last name—keeping the secret of her son's origin.

Jesús Zarate lived.

All these years later she worried about him more than ever. Would he one day dangle for days from a tree, meeting the same fate as three generations of Malverde men—his father, his father and his father before him? Or would Jesús tempt fate, stand against all odds and win? The future seemed deadly. But the future also seemed alive. For now Jesús must face life alone, find the truth within himself. She would disappear tomorrow. That is just what she did.

IT'S ELECTRIC

SWIMMING naked in the wine glass-shaped pool of the Happy Canyon house Dieter Stone rented for the upcoming porn shoot, he and Amber Black dove, came up for air and frolicked. Shining bright blue underwater lights gave the swell of their bare asses the look of wet dolphins surfacing in the ocean.

But all was not well in Happy Canyon.

The Nazi anthem Horst Wessel Lied played on the sound system.

Dieter placed both hands on the pool's smooth tiled edge and hoisted himself with difficulty. Muscle tone had disappeared years ago. All that matched his surname nowadays were gall and kidney stones his doctor said must be removed one day soon.

Still, Stone commanded power.

Standing with drunken difficulty, he dripped, straightened and goose-stepped in all his pale, nude, flabby glory to the electric wine cooler, where eighteen perfectly chilled bottles of chardonnay awaited.

Licking her lips, Amber flipped her long blond ponytail like a pampered mare in heat.

"Stop, Dieter, stop. I can't take it."

Dieter sang along with the rousing words to the Third Reich marching song.

"The flag on high," Dieter said.

Amber giggled a series of high-pitched notes that sounded like off-key piccolo music.

"You must stand at attention and salute the Fatherland, my

little Maus," he said, pointing to his cocked private part.

"You are so naughty, meine Dieter" Amber said.

Squealing with alcohol-induced excitement, she swam to shallow water and walked to the edge on gumball green painted tippy-toes, pedicured to perfection on a weekly basis. Once streamlined and athletic, now puffy and loaded with Zyprexa, Prozac and Cymbalta antidepressant meds, she hauled her damaged frame from the heated pool.

Amber knew her sacrifice would be well worth the trouble if Dieter bought Neverland. After working too hard with no scruples, she'd finally be in the big money. If she kept his little German sausage on her good side, she might even hook up with a couple of those Berlin and Munich porn stars from his movies—real Aryan men who would treat her the way she deserved. And she wouldn't have to placate this pompous swine anymore.

Dieter wanted to bring back MJ's Neverland amusement park to use as his main porn movie setting and do movies with scenes on the merry-go-round, in the little train, and even with the filthy flamingos. Perverts rule. Amber envisioned renting overhung porn actors overpriced canyon houses twelve months of the year.

Dieter stopped marching and offered a stiff-armed salute. Turning to jiggle his genitals, he leered at Amber.

"You want some knockwurst?" he said.

Grabbing a bottle of wine from the electric black and stainless steel cooler, he leaped feet first back into the water, remaining underwater longer than usual until his head finally bobbed to the surface. Dieter opened the wine bottle, took a big swig and handed off to Amber.

"How do you say savage in German," she asked.

"Wilde," Dieter said.

Wally stepped from behind the purple luster of a poolside jacaranda tree.

"Well, look who is it," Dieter said.

"You two only care about yourselves," Wally said. "You don't care about hurting people. I'm not like Michael. You're like Michael. You're not nice. It's nice to be nice."

"Boy, you are one world-class sicko," Dieter said.

"Do something," Amber said.

Struggling, Dieter pulled his frail frame from the water and stood precariously on the pool's rolled tile edge. Wally placed the toe of his left sneaker against the electric wine cooler, nudging just enough to send the whirring machine into the swimming pool. When Dieter grabbed for the cooler, Amber grabbed him.

The splash looked like a cannonball dive at a redneck picnic— a good title and plot, come to think of it, for one of Dieter's porn flicks. "Redneck Picnic."

Come one, come all.

Sparks and flames flew like a July 4th spectacle at a bargain-basement winery— exploding bottle rockets bought from the road-side stand and rancid guzzled Muscatel all part of the red, white and blue holiday celebration.

Wally watched the display with the calm confidence of a sea-soned executioner pulling the switch. As soon as the electric cooler hit the water, already faulty pool lights and an illegal jerry-rigged wiring system blew, sending enough shock waves through the water to electrocute the VIP seating section at a capital punishment convention. Amber's ponytail stood on end. Dieter stiffened from gelled head to toe nails, like a sideshow attraction at the proposed "New Neverland" porn park—Mr. Dickhead, the Human Erection.

Walking to the pool house, Wally shut off the electrical circuit breaker to the pool's lighting and pump systems, unplugged the electric cooler and reached for a long bamboo pole equipped with a rubber cup and cloth sieve Dieter used to fish leaves and other de-bris from the pool. Instead of Cooper's hawk feathers, Wally guided the bobbing bodies to the edge and fished out the warm remains of Dieter and Amber.

"It's electric," Syrah said.

Digging into the right pocket of his jeans, Wally drew his cork-screw. Kneeling, he pushed the sharp silver utensil into the center of Dieter's right eyeball and twisted clockwise. Pushing against the dead man's forehead with his left hand, he pulled with his right. This time the orb came out full, plump, looking like a ripe grape.

Wally scampered to Amber's body, got balanced on his knees, positioned the corkscrew in the center of her right eyeball and twisted clockwise. The fibrous tissue imploded, squishy, mushy, like when you step on a Pacific red snapper fish head on the pier and the eyes pop. This time when Wally pulled, something resembling a little blue marble came with the tug.

"Practice makes perfect," Syrah said.

Wally dropped the corkscrew and the gooey attached glob, turned off the marching music, and headed back to the van.

"Those people drink too much," Syrah said.

"No staying power, either," Wally said. "Central Coast chardonnay drinkers don't seem to have much of a shelf life."

MORE WINE, LESS CHAT

ONE rare rainy Sunday when Wayne was still alive, at 2:27 p.m., three women, one very tall and stern, entered the "Burnt Straw Canyon Winery" tasting room just a few miles northeast of Santa Barbara. Located off a deep canyon road kissed by ocean breezes, surrounded by brown or lush green mountains depending on the season and rolling vineyards puffy with the innate energy of chardonnay, the white queen of California's most planted wine grape, Wayne's weird, wild winery prospered.

The "western" decor of the room accentuated the pseudo-hip assortment of eccentrics, wealthy poseurs and assorted wine highbrows who tasted on each of the seven days the boutique winery operated from morning until night. The tasters were too hip for their own good—so hip it hurt.

Wayne Wilson produced three kinds of chardonnay: creamy unoaked, citrusy unoaked and sparkling chardonnay. All three picked up top-of-the-line awards and, frankly, cost way too much at his wine trail winery. Many people, particularly out-of-state tourists, didn't appreciate or understand Wayne's wine as they window-shopped, no matter how rich they were. With little patience for the uninformed wine palate and suffering wine fools unkindly, the Burnt Straw Canyon Winery staff handled duds and dullards, as well as upscale tourist traffic and coddled LA capitalists.

Wally had been working as a tasting room attendant for about three weeks, still feeling awkward and knowing never to speak to the big boss. Stories of Wayne Wilson's temper loomed large in Santa Barbara. The word "temperamental" should appear on all his wine labels. Wally feared Wayne.

But he was getting smarter about wine, studying the wine lists at night when he went home and developing some pouring skill from watching his co-workers handle customers. Talking was tough but he pushed himself to try to describe the taste, color and process that somehow put grapes in a glass.

Some people actually knew far less than he did about wine in general, let alone chardonnay. In his first week, a man wearing camouflage fatigue pants, a Wayne Newton T-shirt, blue rubber flip flops and a Dodgers' cap on backwards seemed embarrassed to even ask his question. But he asked anyway.

"How do you do it?" he asked.

"Do what?"

"Get the pineapples in?"

"Pineapples?"

"And the baked apples?"

It dawned on Wally that the customer thought winemakers actually stuck whole pineapples and baked apples and who knew what else into the winemaking process from barrel to bottle so the scents hung around to tease the discerning palate and nostrils.

Wally could not have offered a nicer explanation.

"Oh, no, sir," he said. "We don't do that at all. Tastes you hear people talk about are mostly really not there. Taste and fragrance is mostly in your head not in your nose or on your tongue. The hints and notes and fragrances are all pretty much imaginary. The pie crusts and coconuts aren't really pie crusts and coconuts. You invent them. Open yourself to the heavenly grace of the wine."

Holy shit, that one nearly floored Wally—the heavenly grace of the wine.

"Enter the soul of the wine," Wally said.

Wally was getting good.

The man seemed disappointed but relieved.

"I see," he said. "I think."

Had Wally's mother not pushed him to put in an application, he would never have stopped by the tasting room. He liked wine, of course, sweet fruit wines mostly, like Banana Red or Dragon Fruit

20 20 but had no real wine expertise. Mary Jane's bedtime stories when he was little about Boone's Farm apple wine always made him laugh. After Wally lost one menial job after another for the past twenty years, and without any backstory, Mary Jane pushed Wally to the tasting room.

"You have to work, baby," she said. "The doctor says you need structure."

"I'd rather meditate," Wally said. "Zen masters say there's structure in no structure."

"Zen masters aren't wrong," Mary Jane said. "But your doctor says you need medication and meditation."

One of these days, though, Wally planned to stop—the medication, not the meditation.

Although the three women were obviously having a good time on that rare rainy day on the Central Coast, the tallest seemed impatient. Kidding with each other the way good friends do, the women sipped from a 2015 unoaked vintage.

"Wouldn't it be great if it rained chardonnay?" the shortest woman asked.

"You sound like you're dropping acid rather than drinking wet straw," said the woman in the middle.

"Burnt straw, not wet straw," said the tallest woman.

Wally laughed along.

Now he took a deep breath like the yoga teachers on TV said to do when pressure and stress got bad. He wanted to share whatever knowledge he had picked up about wine to help make the women's visit mean something when they returned to Los Angeles. Wally heard them say they worked in the business. Wally knew they must be in the movie business even though he didn't recognize them. Wally felt up to the job. For the first time in a long time, Wally felt confident.

"This wine is a full-bodied unoaked delight," Wally said.

"Awesome," the short woman said.

"We're talking chalking," Wally said.

The women looked puzzled.

"Talking chalking," Wally said. "A textural chalky minerality is delicately apparent in the processing of the grapes."

Wally was outdoing himself, going out on a limb in ramping up descriptions—Wally wild with winsome wine words. Hopefully the women wouldn't ask for details or tell him they were calcite scientists or calcium carbonite experts.

"Turn sideways," Wally said. "Like the wine movie."

The short woman turned.

"You ought to be in pictures." Wally said. "This wine's richer profile of lush tropical fruit matches the fine lines of your profile, your facial structure which matches your nose and the nose of the vine buds."

The woman laughed and started to blush.

Wally was pumped, feeling fine, apple blossom time in the wine business. Maybe this would work out after all. Wally working the wine full-time might be nice.

The taller woman was not impressed.

Weaponizing her words, she blasted Wally's confidence.

"More wine, less chat," she said.

Embarrassed to the point of almost passing out, Wally's normally teetering ego deflated; the blood drained from Wally's face. Pouring three more tasting samples, Wally stood by silently, wearing a cool thin smile. The women tasted as if he wasn't even there.

Syrah spoke up during the drive home that night and wouldn't shut up.

"More wine, less chat," she said. "More wine, less chat."

Shrieking like a kidnapped parrot from an old pirate's home, Syrah relentlessly repeated how the world needed fewer mean-spirited people who needed to disappear as soon as possible.

"Might as well throw those stupid business cards away," Syrah said. "They say, 'Wally Zook, Tasting Room Attendant,' like you're a men's room attendant handing out towels to make the pee pee dribbles disappear."

Wally teared up, reached under the dash and threw his box of cards out the Subaru window.

"By the way, Wally," Syrah said. "You're nicer when you're not taking your meds. I like you just the way you are. I don't like it when chemistry comes between us."

Even though Wally told his mother all the details of his humiliation, Mary Jane made Wally go back to work at the winery the next day.

"You have to keep working, sweetie," his mother said at breakfast. "Your shifts at the winery will help you get better, will help you heal. You want to heal, don't you?"

"I need new business cards," Wally said. "But I don't want people to think I'm the men's room attendant."

Mary Jane poured herself a jelly jar full of Syrah when she finished her granola.

"Good choice, mom," Syrah said. "Red-blooded wine for a red-blooded woman."

PARTIAL TO PINOT

"I'M partial to pinot," Rose said. "I like pinot noir because it's lighter; a little less alcohol than the big reds."

Reaching for the brown paper bag that held the bottle on the dresser in their room at the Sea Urchin Inn in Shell Beach, Rose used a gnawed thumbnail to peel the foil from the glass neck.

"We don't have a corkscrew," she said.

Wallace pulled off a steel-toed motorcycle boot, slid the bottle inside bottom down and slammed the heel and non-skid rubber sole against the wall. Within two minutes of pounding, he reached into the black boot and pulled the cork from the bottle.

"Where'd you learn that trick?" Rose asked.

"Two weeks at skinhead summer camp for five years, from when I was 10 to when I was 15."

"There's really such a thing as skinhead summer camp?"

"In Bakersfield. The three guys who ran it said they were professional martial artists, ex-Special Forces and SEALS, but we didn't believe them. They were pretty much just violent drunks. Taught us how to shoot, though, how to give ourselves stitches if we got cut, put together homemade bombs, fight with hunting knives, and do secret ninja moves. How to hate people who needed hating was what we learned best, though."

Rose filled two plastic bathroom cups with an earthy Laetitia pinot noir.

"You really hate as many people as you say you do?" she asked.

"I think so but don't know for sure."

"Who exactly do you hate?"

"Mexicans and Muslims, for starters."

"All the LGBTQ letters, too, I'll bet," she said.

"In every language."

"Liberals?"

"Libtard mental disorder."

"Who do you like?" she asked.

"White people. White is right."

"Jesus Christ.'

"Yeah, I hate him, too. Long-haired Jew bastard," Wallace said.

"I was just cursing, not asking if you hated the Lord. You are some lost cause, Mr. President of the Crushers Motorcycle Club."

"We're both lost causes. And don't call me that, anymore. I told you, the club is dead."

"Think they know we're together?"

"They know."

"What do we do?" Rose asked.

"Your call."

"What do you mean?"

"We're on our own. We either split up or travel together."

Rose looked into the cranberry hues of her pinot noir.

"You think we can pull this off?"

Wallace looked into his empty cup.

"I mean the whole thing, getting out, being together, staying sane," Rose said.

"I'm not sane, Rose."

"What do you mean?"

I have issues. I served in combat in Afghanistan. I'm supposed to be taking medicine and seeing the doctor at the VA but I don't like the way the pills make me feel and I don't like the way the doctor makes me feel. I threw them both out last week."

"You threw the doctor out?"

"Almost threw him out the fifth floor window at the hospital. I held him out the window by his ankles for about a minute. Then I pulled him back in. Told him I was kidding. Just to teach him a lesson. I think there's a warrant out for me. The doctor wanted to give me morphine suppositories. Stick opium up my ass? The Taliban didn't even think of that. The doctor definitely got the wrong soldier. There should be a warrant out for him."

"Jesus Christ."

"I told you. Fuck him."

"What about us? You want to dangle me out the window some-day, too?"

Wallace lit a Lucky.

"You hate women, too?" Rose asked.

Wallace looked at the pink wall painting that highlighted the inside of a conch shell and quickly looked away.

"I think I hate everybody."

"Can we try some love?" she asked.

"Did I tell you that my mother named me after George Wal-lace?"

Wallace and Rose kissed in the blue shadow of the small televi-sion set tuned to KCOY in Santa Maria.

"Tonight's lead story," the anchor said. "Double firebombing in Lompoc."

"I can't believe the Crushers firebombed both our apartments and we saw it on the 11 o'clock news," Rose said when the live report ended.

"Within an hour of us leaving Dope's," Wallace said. "You know how the boys react."

Rose fell asleep clutching her Smith & Wesson beneath her pillow.

Wally slept with a KA-BAR knife between his legs. If he rolled over the wrong way during the night, at least he knew how to stitch an open wound in his nuts.

CORKSCREWED

Jesús Zarate, 45, observed his female co-workers in the Santa Maria Mirror newsroom the way a microbiologist watches germs in a petri dish. What brain misfire caused young women to get tattoos on their feet? The copy editor wore a dark green lizard, the education reporter sported an orange monarch butterfly and the features editor displayed a fat red and black ladybug.

Standing by the break room microwave, Jesús heated water for green tea.

"Tell your daughters not to tattoo their feet. The colors will fade one day and look like ink blot tests your psychiatrists will use to figure out what's wrong with you getting tats on your feet in the first place," he said.

"Fuck you, Zarate."

"Mind your own business, asshole."

"I'm filing a complaint with human resources."

"Don't blame the messenger," Jesús said. "I'm doing it for the children."

Jesús wore his own tattoo on his left upper arm, vivid, multicolored ink that bore the bold likeness of Mexican folk hero Jesús Malverde. Quick to tell anybody brave or stupid enough to ask about the likeness that Malverde is more powerful than God, Jesús' affinity for his personal saint was born of the same love and respect he held for his mother. Zita prayed to Malverde, the Mexican Robin Hood, every morning when she awoke and every night before she went to bed.

But she never shared her secret.

Malverde came to Jesús in a dream one night about six months after his mother disappeared for no reason and left such a powerful impression that he found out as much as he could about the "Narco-Saint" before getting the tattoo that covered his left shoulder and snaked its way almost to his elbow. Narco-traffickers had hijacked Malverde from the campesinos. But the poor and the pious knew the super saint belonged to them. Jesús felt a familiar affinity he could not explain, that Malverde particularly belonged to him.

The tattoo of Malverde's head loomed large with a bright red bandana inked around the neck of an open-necked white shirt complete with black epaulets, patch pockets and the blackest ink for Santos Malverde's hair, eyebrows and moustache as well as the pitch-dark pools of his eyes.

The great man died May 3, 1909, hanged by the rich from a tree in Culiacan, Mexico. No one had ever mentioned Jesús' father to him, but for some reason Jesús believed the mystery man was born and raised in that same city.

Confusion often comes from a bad dream—a reoccurring nightmare from which you cannot escape. Bewilderment clouded Jesús' mind every time he thought about his father. If he asked, perhaps Malverde would help him unravel the mystery. Maybe Malverde would take him under his wing and advise him.

Most men in the newsroom, particularly the young reporters, kept their distance.

How the hell Jesús was supposed to write news columns in this nursery school environment was beyond him. With the exception of his editor, experienced newsroom managers were bureaucratic hacks, clerks of fact who didn't care for a middle-aged outlaw journalist in their midst.

Most new breed reporters were happy dancing millennial zombies entering deeper and deeper into the attention-deficit twilight zone of devices—smart phones in their hands, buds in their ears, distracted and chatting on computer screens while writing their flat stories at the same time. Whatever happened to focus? Whatever happened to two-fisted, hard-drinking newspaper people who took bad news seriously?

"What are you working on?" Jesús' editor asked, standing behind him and looking over his shoulder.

"Don't read my shit until it's done," Jesús said. "It's bad luck."

Jesús knew his share of bad luck.

On the day his mother vanished police took the missing person's report but showed no real interest short of insinuating Jesús had something to do with the disappearance. Nobody in the neighborhood seemed to have any idea where she could have gone. If they did, nobody was talking.

Six months later, after working under the table as a bar bouncer in upscale and not-so-upscale clubs, he bought a flat black 1963 Lincoln Continental lowrider from a dead drug dealer's wife, with a killer hydraulic lift system to produce super hopping, red leather interior and suicide doors. Rolling out of the barrio on 20-inch wheels with state-of-the art white low profile tires, Jesús drove this dark bullet three hours north up the 101 to get out of the city and settle in quiet Santa Maria agribusiness strawberry country with his cousin, Palita.

Cops said they'd let him know if they came up with any leads about his mother.

They didn't.

Within a year Jesús beat a guy to death in the West Main Street parking lot of a sleazy unlicensed social club and did 8 years of a 10 year prison sentence in the San Luis Men's Colony. Keeping a daily journal, Jesús learned to write clean and tight copy in the penitentiary, penning a weekly column in the prison newspaper. A real newspaper job came after his release when he saved a visiting publishing executive from a street mugging by members of "Los Matadores," a West Side Santa Maria gang. "Life is a long story," Jesús wrote in his introductory Santa Maria Mirror news column and regularly told the pests he encountered along the way—people who wasted his time digging for motivation into his behavior.

"You really using corkscrewed as a verb?" the editor said.

"You ought to use it in the headline," Jesús said.

"A little rough, don't you think?"

"Corkscrewing the wine baron's eyeball isn't rough?"

A dull police reporter wrote the typical lifeless front page story. Jesús handled the meat and potatoes of color, narrative mystery and his signature touch that made readers either love him or hate him. This tale of woe and brutality would garner both reactions—hatred from the vintners, the tourist associations and the powerful money mongers, and love from those who craved the hardboiled true crime tales in which Jesús specialized.

"Your eyeball weighs about an ounce, by the way," Jesús said.

"Any suspects?" his editor asked.

"Like maybe everybody. The guy was a world-class jerkoff who made world-class chardonnay who wound up getting a world-class screwing. His homicide gives new meaning to the wine industry word 'body'."

"Brut, too," the editor said.

"Hey, that's pretty good. How about 'Brut Corkscrews Wine Baron's Body' as my column headline?" Jesús asked.

Afraid to laugh, the editor kept a straight face and went into his office. Jesús gave the poor bastard two years in the job. Like others Jesús encountered he wouldn't last and was better suited selling coastal real estate.

When Jesús finished the column, he moved the piece from his personal file to the local news file so his editor could read and clear the piece for the paper. Jesús could go home in about a half hour. The editor rarely asked questions about his columns which was good. Jesús hated discussing changes or making even slight compromises. Artificial editors got on his nerves. Because of them the glory days of authentic local news columnists were coming to a close.

After a decade living on the outside as a model citizen, he was by anybody's standards a veteran newspaper columnist, an ex-convict killer but a journalism award-winner, too, a pro who was very good at what he did. The editors and reporters knew it, too, which caused resentment within their ranks. For the most part Jesús rolled alone.

Only a handful of bosses backed him up over the years. Most editors and publishers were stiffs—the worst of the lot giving him column writing advice when they had never written a news column in their lives or, if they had, never banged one out good enough to keep people talking at work, in the bar or at home at the dinner table.

A writing coach once showed up in the newsroom and the editor asked Jesús to talk with her. When the coach stopped by his desk, he said he had a deal for her—read twelve of his columns and then they would talk. If she only read one or two, she'd miss his essence, what he saw and how he saw it. She'd miss the consistency of his values, the fine line of justice that traced its name on every paragraph. If he wasn't worth the time it took her to read a dozen columns, she wasn't worth his time to talk. Jesús and the coach never spoke again.

On another day a sociopathic executive editor unleashed an insecure managing editor on him, saying the man would help Jesús become a better columnist. The guy was a wannabe news columnist himself who Jesús saw as having zero originality and a severe testicular deficit when it came to agitating and starting shit that any true columnist has the day-to-day solemn responsibility to start.

Spreading truth and light on the frontier meant taking risks. Awakening the sleeping minds of people on the raw western edge of America constituted more calling than job. Writing three good news columns a week—and on special occasions such as deadline murders, killer mudslides and ocean body searches—wasn't rocket science but most good daily journalists couldn't pull it off.

Sadly, most people he met in Santa Maria showed pathetic indifference to news. They took it. They left it. But after his first two years, Jesús left them hooked and wanting more. He addicted wealthy sots, too, drunk on power, business and ego, whining and wanting less. But he got their attention. Who did this LA Chicano ex-con think he was showing up on the beach for a fatal great white shark attack in a deep purple double-breasted suit and huaraches? Asking the judges how much they got paid because he wanted to publish their salaries in the paper to see if readers wanted them to give the money back? Asking why city cops didn't arrest a machete murderer 50 witnesses at a beer party in the park saw kill a Mexican teenager?

Jesús's Sunday column showed up marked "read" in twenty minutes. Grabbing his black leather briefcase, he didn't say good-bye to anyone when he left, walked through the sweet fragrance of night blooming jasmine, and slid into the low-rider Lincoln.

This wine murder was a big murder. All the PR flacks from LA would be rushing into California's "other" wine country to try to get a piece of the damage control action. Napa to the north was known as primo Cali grape land, but the Central Coastal rep was coming up fast. People with big money were vying to take the lead. A lot rested on a regional reputation of safe, not sorry, when you came to drink the chardonnay.

Aikido class at the Grover Beach dojo started at 7. Jesús didn't want to be late for the dynamic harmony of the self-defense he so much desired and needed more than a good corkscrewing. Without practicing the rough roots of peace, no one, especially Jesús, could say when he would lose it, snap and kill again. If that happened, he could kiss his own life goodbye as well.

Giving peace a chance made sense.

WATER IN A WINE GLASS

HARD memories die hardest.

Working the winery, Wally did his best to adapt to the surroundings of his new career. The cash register was a particularly major obstacle because he had never worked in a fast food restaurant or retail store of any kind. Wally was a manual labor guy—yard work, pool work and errands of every kind, including a recent old-fashioned ditch digging job that embarrassed him when the other laborers made kissing sounds at passing young women.

But no cash registers, which were really computers which Wally didn't own or use unless you counted his cell phone which was basic and too complicated for him to understand.

If that wasn't bad enough, now he was watching a seven-year-old Shirley Temple look-alike come bouncing butterscotch curls into the house of chardonnay.

"I'm a big girl," she said.

Wally looked around for help.

"Oh, yes, you are a big girl," said the man striding big daddy steps right behind her.

"Our great big, beautiful doll," said the woman holding the child's hand.

Pulling a high wooden stool away from the short tasting bar, the girl's father placed both hands on his daughter's hips and hoisted her to her seat. Crisp petticoat ruffles scraped against sharp creases of an expensive purple velvet dress better suited for a private elementary school musical.

The child crossed her ankles with the practiced ease she

learned during a week at "Missy Manners" charm school in Laguna Hills.

"And what would you like to taste today?" Wally asked the adults.

Doing his best to ignore the child at the bar, he looked into her parents' eyes and placed two long-stemmed wine glasses in front of the woman and the man.

"Three wine glasses," the man said.

Wally didn't move. Before he could explain that children are not allowed to drink and probably should not even sit at the bar, the man dismissed him with a wave of his hand.

"Margot will have her sparkling water in a wine glass," he said.

"With a cherry," Margot said.

"We'll taste the 2009 Perky Chardonnay, the 2010 Honors Chardonnay and the 2011 Ribbon Chardonnay," the woman said.

Wally ignored the water order and poured two fingers of the 2009 vintage into two glasses.

"Here's to good company," he said.

The woman rolled her eyes.

"Please pour Margot's 2009 faux chardonnay," she said.

When Wally began to object, the man put on a stern face and slid his hand to the side of his mouth, preventing Margot from lip reading the words her daddy spoke to Wally in a harsh whisper.

"Margot likes to do what Mommy and Poppy do," he said in a hiss.

The tasting room manager appeared.

"Is there something I can help with here?" she asked.

Wally pointed to the child.

"Well, well, well," the manager said to Margot. "Thank you for visiting our boutique winery. Please give me a moment, Miss."

Darling Margot folded her hands as if she were in prayer. Gilded fingernails polished gold twinkled in the dazzling sunlight that filtered through stained glass windows that lined the tasting room.

Lifting an empty bottle of Perky from the bar, the manager rushed to the sink and washed out the bottle three times—once in very hot water, once in lukewarm water and once in cold water.

Draining the bottle for the last time, she dabbed at the green glass mouth with a clean white cloth and filled the bottle with sparkling water from an expensive brand she took from a cooler and opened. The manager poured fresh sparkling water into Margot's wine glass.

Lifting her drink, Margot pushed her nose into the glass and sniffed. Poppy clapped his hands. Mommy took a picture on her cell. Poppy shot a video on his phone. Mommy took another shot of Margot. Now Mommy shot a selfie with Margot as they both posed, daintily holding their wine glass stems while making pouty, flirty kissy faces.

Wally wanted to kill the whole family—winery manager included.

Bongos pounded so hard in his head his eyeballs vibrated.

BEING ALIVE AND KNOWING IT

SITTING zazen in full lotus never caused cramps or even minor discomfort for Wally. Seasoned sitters sometimes lost all feeling in their legs and keeled over when trying to stand after a particularly grueling session of seated meditation.

Not Wally.

Maybe that's why the whole idea of zazen appealed to him—sitting quietly doing nothing—although he readily acknowledged fear of whatever might lurk in the small recess of his big dark mind, especially now that Syrah's chattering interrupted him whenever she chose, particularly when he needed quiet calm and stillness.

Japanese Zen Buddhism in America appealed to Wally ever since Mary Jane took to sitting beneath the palm fronds in her backyard. She seemed so peaceful there. But monkey mind, as the monks—no relation to monkeys—called it in the monasteries he read about, jumping from tree to tree, from branch to branch before climbing higher or falling into the gaping mouth of the beast—in his mind always a tiger—rattled him.

So Wally promised himself he'd sit every morning before hitting the road in the van wherever he happened to sleep, which had become an increasing problem with all the "No Overnight Parking" signs posted up and down the coastal highways and even in the towns and cities. Supermarket parking lots usually provided refuge and seemingly appealed to the growing small army of men and women of all ages on the road. Wally liked employee parking lots—visitor parking, in fact—at newspapers or television stations. He could usually roll in and roll out before anybody noticed he was there or questioned his business. A uniformed private security guard with a gun once asked and Wally said the station was doing a story about him and his bus.

"Cool, dude," the guard said.

With nicer weather and the abundance of despair wracking people's lives all over the country, the Central Coast beckoned those who came in a used RV or camper attached to a pickup truck and at night parked wherever they could. Sometimes people came to kill themselves while in the death grip of mental terror, choosing a bucolic place by the ocean to end it all. One last breath of ocean air felt like a final treat.

Wally wanted to blow his mind, not blow his brains out—at least not yet.

The pull-out bed in the bus was perfect for meditation meant to erase winery flashbacks and create a mind of no mind. Wally just closed the curtains over the jalousie windows, folded his legs like a pretzel, placed the tops of his left fingers into the palm of his right hand, connected his thumbs and tilted his head forward so his half-closed eyes focused on the floor. Inhaling slowly and deeply, he mindfully tried to feel every moment of every breath as he reached the top and then slowly exhaled, reversing the process before doing it all over again.

Zen enlightenment simply meant being alive and knowing it.

Wally vowed to sit for 30 minutes each morning and hoped in the near future to work his way up to a second session at night before bed. Zazen made body and mind good to go for the circle of life that led one day into the next. When the circle stopped, you stopped. No breath, no ki, no vital life energy.

The dead end awaited everybody.

"Wake up," Syrah said.

"That's what the Zen masters say," Wally said.

"No, I mean wake up, you comatose Howdy Doody dipshit. Time to get moving. I'm tired of trying to stay one step ahead of keeping the cops from rousting us. You really don't want to be drawing attention to us, anyway. If you know what I mean."

"I was studying myself, alive and aware," Wally said. "I was not asleep."

"Guess those two lovebirds floating in the swimming pool weren't dead either."

Wally rubbed his eyes and tried to focus. What was she talking about? He had no idea where Syrah was coming from. She was starting to unnerve and bother him when he depended on her more and more for friendship and the courage just to get up in the morning.

Unwinding toothpick pale legs, Wally stretched and wriggled his bare toes. Wearing his jeans and a purple tie-dyed T-shirt with a unicorn imprint in the middle of his chest, he pushed back the curtains, twisted open the window slats, and caught a scent of eucalyptus from century-old trees that stood with great dignity near the road. Opening the double doors, Wally stepped outside, feeling gravel beneath his bare feet.

"This is great," he said.

"We'll see how great it is when the California Highway Patrol, the Santa Barbara Sheriff's Department and any available SWAT team unit figures out what you did and who you are," Syrah said. "That newspaper communist is calling you the 'Corkscrew Killer' and the 'Central Coastal Corkscrewer.' "

"You're just trying to upset me," Wally said. "You can't scare me, though. I'm free."

"That's what worries me," Syrah said. "Freedom of fear can rule the world—for better or worse."

"I'm going to meditate some more, Syrah. Then we'll get going."

"Knock yourself out, Wally. Lose your mind."

"Don't mind if I do," he said.

TWO FEWER EYEBALLS

DRESSED in a crisp, pleated hakama, the long black dress of the Samurai, and a white martial arts gi top, Jesús easily slipped the punch, reaching, blending and grabbing the attacker's right wrist with his left hand. Helping along the aggression directed at his head, he passed the wrist into his right hand, nudged the attacker's right elbow with his left palm, and stepped under the arm now securing his grip with both hands as if holding a sharp Japanese katana, the death-giving sword of the ancient warrior class. With the attacker's arm now outstretched and pressure building on the elbow, Jesús balanced the cranked shoulder, elbow and wrist over his right shoulder and stopped moving.

"This is the difference between war and peace," he said.

Advanced aikido class students watched silently from the dojo mat.

Extending his outstretched arms, Jesús sensed pain beginning to build in his attacker, the panic beginning to crawl into his brain, the urge to flee building in his heart.

"If I cut down hard, his arm breaks maybe in a few places," Jesús said. "If I drop him with love, with gentle control, he lives without a fracture or two or three. Try it. But be careful. Your partner trusts you."

Ranked as sandan, a third-degree black belt in both aikido and the combat application called aikijujutsu, Jesús trained hard for a decade to achieve proficiency in the arts. Learning not to punch was difficult but worth the effort. Specializing in bone breaks and dislocations, Jesús taught that non-violence is the way until it isn't.

The attacker dictates the dance to be performed, he said. Dish out only as much pain as necessary, he said. Love is always better.

Jesús helped out the school by teaching once a week when his teacher attended Bible study. Jesús lived as a "street Buddhist," taking life as it came to him while his teacher had bounced from Jew to Shinto to born-again Christian. Different strokes for different folks, Jesús told him when he shared his conversion with the class. Jesús liked and respected his teacher, kidding that Jesus of Nazareth was Gautama Buddha's little brother.

Jesús dug diverse California—so many different Californias existing within the whole. Other parts of the big state left him wanting more, better, different. Jesús had grown up a little too late. Eight years in prison, including almost two in the hole for fighting in the yard, didn't help much, either. Haight-Asbury had disappeared in the 60s dream. Snug 50s surf towns like Pismo Beach held on as long as they could but succumbed to developers and builders who always wanted more. Oblivious skaters wearing board brand imprinted beanies and backward baseball caps pulled over their ears joined know-it-all millennials who weren't willing to pay any dues. Together they jammed sidewalks and bars in a rush of shallow daydreaming. Even outlaw bikers weren't what they used to be; some even wore shorts. Short pants on a Hells Angel or Mongol or Crusher was simply too much.

Peace was the answer, of course. But try teaching nonviolence to anybody anymore. Fighting created monsters. Consumer craving for live mixed martial arts, shared video carnage among teenagers on social media, internet video game mayhem, and general acceptance of cruelty as entertainment fueled more assaults, attacks and brutality that created gaps in human thinking that might never heal.

Jesús bemoaned the escalation of simple stupidity that embraced the madness of ignorance. Rather than ratcheting down anxiety the masses of asses cranked up fear. That's why he practiced aikido and aikijujutsu—yin and yang—fighting and not fighting, stressing aikido as the way of peace and harmony, as O'Sensei, the old man who invented the Japanese art, called the practice. With the brutal efficiency of aikijujutsu at the killing art root of sweet dynamic aikido, the abundant peace of aikido could separate some shoulders but still save the world.

After practice, Jesús bowed out, left the mat, checked his phone and immediately called his editor.

"What now?" he asked.

"Two more bodies," the editor said. "Two fewer eyeballs."

The editor quickly filled him in on the details.

"Sonofabitch, I'm on my way," Jesús said.

"No, that's okay," the editor said. "I wanted to tell you to stay put just in case you heard something."

"Stay put?"

"Paige says to tell you we don't need you here tonight."

The phone went dead. Jesús knew it took a half hour to get back to the paper in Santa Maria. He was there in fifteen minutes. Publisher Paige Pennington greeted him at the door wearing a buckskin jacket and a smeared lipstick grin.

"No need to rush, Mr. Zarate," she said.

Jesús smelled wine on her breath.

Posing in a straw cowboy hat and a baked potato-toned tan, she called herself "a California girl." At 50, the women's liberation movement continued to pass her by. An aspiring, yet failed, rodeo queen since she was sixteen, Paige rode sleek horses, never made waves unless she was posing for selfies at the beach, and attended all the Elks Club business gatherings, sucking down tri-tip barbecue and boasting about how much she cared for her little city community. Meanwhile, Paige and her ilk mostly detested the 75 percent majority Mexican population and their offspring unless local business employed them at less than minimum wage with no workplace protection.

"What's the story?" Jesús asked.

"Actually, there is no story," Paige said. "We're pulling your column because we don't want to create any more panic. Your first column induced apoplexy in our vintner community. We don't have enough facts for you to draw any conclusions."

"I conclude that two more corpses with two fewer eyeballs add to the facts," he said. "Homicide can be a real sight for sore eyes, if you catch my drift."

Paige Pennington winced.

"You see?" she said. "That kind of smug assessment of our community gets us nowhere."

Jesús laughed.

"That's my point," he said. "We better see what our readers can't."

"No," the publisher said. "I mean see how you treat these matters? Matters best left unsaid and unwritten. You always add fuel to the fire."

"We're a newspaper, right?"

"Yes, we are, Mr. Zarate."

"And I'm a newspaper columnist."

"For now you are," she said.

Jesús thought peaceful thoughts. But all he could see were three squishy eyeballs leaking from mushy sockets drilled with a sharp and pointy object. Jesús tried but could not get the word "corkscrewed" out of his mind.

"These conclusions are already confirmed by my sources: Three killed in two separate incidents. Eyeballs missing from one wine millionaire, one real estate broker to the stars and one neo-Nazi smut purveyor. That's some local news column, don't you think? Sounds like front page material to me and a column a day for at least a week."

"This is not our kind of community news," Paige said. "Let other media outlets and papers sensationalize all that. We have a responsibility to report what makes life better on the Central Coast, not worse. We cover rodeo parades and our dear little farm children riding sheep in competitions until they're bucked off, cry and puke their little guts out from fear; that's what helps them grow up to be the kind of strong Santa Maria men and women we can count on. That's what makes our lives better here. Your kind of murder coverage makes life worse, Mr. Zarate. Your kind of reality is simply counterproductive and, frankly, very bad for advertising."

Jesús spotted his editor peeking through the newsroom window.

"You're a treasure, Mr. Zarate," the publisher said. "But you really don't understand our take on the news business. Take a few days off to settle down."

"Terrified children mutton busting at your favorite rodeo is child abuse," Jesús said. "Strapping little kids on the backs of sheep until they cry in fear and get thrown is fucked up. Murder is very, very real. Journalism tells the truth. We help make people's lives better and help make good citizens out of children and adults by facing facts. You know what else?"

Paige glared.

"You're not going to make rodeo queen this year, either," Jesús Zarate said.

CATCH A NEW WAVE

"**S**URF'S up, Wallace."

Rose pulled the sheet off her sleeping beauty buddy. Running naked into the bathroom trailing the sheet with Wallace on her tail, Rose leaned against the door as he pushed gently, moving her, as strong as she was. When she relented, he slid between the door and the jamb to take her into his arms. Wallace kissed Rose gently on the side of her head.

"Dude, I'm not kidding about the surf," she said. "We're going surfing."

"I don't surf," Wallace said. "I ride a bike. Bikers don't surf."

"Think you're too tough? Surfing's tougher."

"Rose, I don't know how."

"I'll teach you."

Wallace relented.

Pismo's no cranking surf beach but it's still unpredictable. Within an hour after renting boards and wet suits they were both up and amped on the north side of the pier. Getting up on the board was easier than Wallace expected. A good athlete who excelled in running, skinhead boxing and precision brick throwing at summer camp, Wallace showed good balance and the courage required to stay in a wave.

Rose was a natural.

For her growing up in Republican Temecula had been the best. On San Diego weekends, surfing defined fun. Rose excelled on the board. Strong waves nurtured her most natural instincts. Wind, waves and life in general offered nirvana, molding her attitude about her developing self-identity. God-fearing Christian parents loved her and she loved them back.

Still dressed in her cheerleader's uniform, she snorted her first line of methamphetamine at 17 with her favorite Filipino cornerback after a high school football game. Whatever guardian angels looked over her disappeared and died. Left alone with a diabolical longing for chemical-induced kicks and overdosing on paranoia, an unhinged seductive environment blossomed in her head, tempered only by strong lust for more.

Devils came to party. Demons came to stay. Darkness lit her life.

When she finally fell six months later rehab seemed to last forever. So she split, moving to Oxnard with her dealer, disappearing from the life she led and the people who cared most about her. After that Rose never went home because getting high made sense, even after the dealer died from an overdose after shooting crank into the center of the red heart tattoo he wore on his neck—a heart with Rose's name in the middle.

Getting high still made sense. But the surfboard ruled. All Rose needed was to drag a board into the ocean, catch a wave and enter bliss in the endless empty space between deep water and azure sky. Singing along to the radio she carried everywhere as a teenager, Rose always turned up the volume whenever she heard a new beach tune.

"Catch a wave. Catch a new wave," a teenage Rose once sang at the top of her lungs.

The radio long gone, any notion of fun disappeared as well. Maybe Wallace could make life happen again. Maybe Rose would catch that new wave after all.

Wallace and Rose rode the last wave of the day like a magic carpet from the beginning of time arriving to pick them up and spirit them off to a blessed star-crossed future. Stepping off the board, Rose seemed to bounce when her feet touched the sand. Wallace ran off his sled leaving prints that quickly disappeared when water filled his tracks.

"You did good, hard ass," Rose said. "C'mon, I'll buy you a drink."

In twenty minutes, after returning the boards and wet suits, Rose and Wallace sat tight against each other in Zip's Nightclub &

Beach Bar, drinking Pacificos with back-up shots of tequila.

"I can do this twice," Wallace said. "I can handle two beers and two shots. Then I need to eat."

"I'm good for two, too," Rose said. "I want to party until two o'clock closing time."

Wallace knew she was serious.

"It's three in the afternoon, Rose."

"You want to dance, little lady?" the man said.

Wallace looked up to see black wraparound shades and a shaved head, a red and black checked flannel shirt buttoned to the neck of a weaving drunk with beer foam on his moustache and nostrils leaning in, already too close to Rose who looked up at the same time.

"No thanks," she said.

"You sure pretty, Mami," the drunk said. My name is Hector. I'm from Bakersfield."

Shaking his head, Wallace stood, looking to the bar for assistance and thinking that he'd never escape Bakersfield. It was like skinhead camp was haunting him, following him wherever he went. The bartender and waitress mixed drinks, carried beers and didn't see—or want to see—what was cooking.

Wallace did not need this shit. Hector was beyond rational. Even sober the guy was no doubt more than a haywire handful. Wallace didn't want to hit him for a number of reasons and had no idea what Rose might do. In the month or so he had known her from the diner she always kept her cool and operated with a sharp chip on her shoulder that never stopped her from doing her job. But she finally snapped on Animal. That took guts and she was under more pressure now. Maybe Wallace should hit this Bakersfield homeboy anyway. Getting pissed, he hadn't even ordered a drink. His stomach growled.

The goon moved slowly toward Wallace, who stepped back to wind up for a move of his own, when what looked like a large shadow swept in from nowhere; a big man in a long ponytail seemed to glide as he stepped into the middle of the clash.

"Thank you for asking, vato. I'd love to dance," the shadow said.

When the bruiser threw a looping right hand, the good Samaritan moved in a wide swooping circle, catching the man's wrist on the outside with his right hand, grabbing and dragging the arm down toward the dance floor. In the same motion he reached with his left hand and got a snug grip behind the man's shirt collar. Then he started to spin, fast and clockwise, using the attacker's momentum to bring him around almost full circle. Rising now, he caught the man hard with his right palm under his chin. Extending both arms, he sent the man airborne into the street before the body settled sprawled and damaged on the sidewalk, landing with a herky-jerky spasm.

Hector passed out unmoving in a warm puddle of piss and Pismo afternoon cool.

The ejection happened fast; the bartender and server still didn't notice.

Never breaking a sweat the stranger returned to the table.

"Just like the movies," Rose said, using a flip flopped bare big toe to nudge her beach bag under the table. The heavy metal bulk of her 9 mm. semi-automatic, fourteen-shot clip with one in the chamber, fluorescent night sighted Smith & Wesson helped her feel confident, secure and a bit unhinged.

Deferring to Wallace, the man extended his right hand.

"Jesús Zarate," he said.

"Like karate?" Rose said.

Jesús smiled.

"No," he said. "More like swing dancing."

THE SMELL OF STRAWBERRIES

STRAWBERRIES bigger than golf balls grow year round in fertile Santa Maria fields. About a dozen varieties flourish in the cool night air and dazzling sunshine of this perfect climate, a valley of sugary, juicy fruit, grueling hard work and money made of sweat and abuse.

The agribusiness farmers tell you they love their workers. What they love is the work the Mexicans provide, the loyalty the mostly undocumented workers offer. But the self-professed stewards of the land love the proceeds best, the fruits of others' labors, far more than they care for the people or the fruit itself.

Nobody loved the smell of strawberries more than Carlos Delgado.

"Ladies and Gentlemen, it is with great honor that I present the next governor of California," said Republican Santa Maria Mayor Sammy Delgado, Carlos' younger brother.

The Elks Club banquet room erupted with applause. Delgado oozed warmth walking through the room shaking hands, kissing women and making his way to the dais where he would deliver his first campaign speech of the year. Women in Western-style dresses and polished cowboy boots opened their mouths wide to cheer. Men in open necked dress shirts and blue sport coats, as well as the occasional pair of new blue jeans and straw cowboy hat, leaped to their feet for a standing ovation.

Santa Maria Mirror Publisher Paige Pennington, seated at the first row of tables, caught a powerful and lingering whiff of the strong strawberry aftershave lotion Delgado manufactured and splashed daily on his smooth tawny cheeks, a scent that defined him more than his calling card, his credit card, babies in two countries and his uncontrollable zest for profit.

A small bottle of "Fresa Te Amo" adorned every table—retail cost $12 a bottle, which according to recent sales statistics should sell for less than three dollars. Macho Mexican men refused to walk around smelling like fruity fields where mostly indigenous women worked—short, strong, Oaxacans who hailed from an ancient culture very different from anywhere else in the spacious Mexican state.

The strawberry pickers didn't speak Spanish for the most part. More than sixteen languages in Oaxaca, starting with Mixtec, Zapotec and so many others coupled with local dialects, shape the conversations and expression of the native people who live there. Subjected to a well-established bigoted pecking order, with too many Mexicans from other parts of the country picking on and mocking Oaxacans, mimicking the jabbering cadence of their voices and the isolated independence of their deeply-rooted identities, the Oaxacans persevered.

So Delgado sold his scent to customers in the agricultural business, white, privileged farmers and their whiter privileged sons, tractor salesmen and the other kiss asses—narrow-minded Swiss Italian cops and firefighters, tiresome elected officials who claimed to be descendants of Spanish immigrants as far back as the conquistadores and worse—who gathered for regular brainless events that served as nothing more than self-congratulatory dinners and award ceremonies.

Tonight at the Elks was no different. But tonight was bigger and better, because Delgado, if elected governor, would skim the cream from the strawberries and keep it here in his hometown, mostly in his own pocket, of course, with some candy-coated spill for the men and women who served him and his business interests, including the cologne market and the property owners who produced the crops. Holding his hands above his head like a welterweight fighter, Delgado's teeth gleamed. Stepping to the mike he bowed his head. The room fell silent.

"Heavenly Father," he said. "I thank you for your blessing on these fine people and on this fine occasion. I thank you for the seeds of life. I thank you for your love."

"Sounds like an endorsement from above," the Elks Club president said.

Delgado dropped the mike, laughing for what seemed like five minutes, showing the polished porcelain of fine caps, a carved jawline and not a single gray hair out of place. Even God took second place when Delgado stepped into a Santa Maria banquet room.

"Brothers and sisters, thank you," Delgado said, touching his palm to his crisp starched shirt and patting his heart. "Tonight we share a meal and give thanks. Tomorrow we announce the official campaign kickoff in the fields, where my sainted parents picked strawberries, where I picked strawberries, where I stooped in labor for so long I never thought I would rise again. But I rose. We rose. Together we will take the mansion in Sacramento and move it here to Santa Maria, our All-American city," he said.

Whoops, barks and whistles followed. Leaning over her chardonnay, Paige whispered wine breath smelling of avarice, hints of hatefulness and a bouquet of miserableness into rodeo board chairman Buck Steward's ear.

"I'll order Zarate to write a column tomorrow about the field campaign announcement," Paige said. "He can open by describing the plump strawberries. Close with tonight's heavenly endorsement."

"Sounds like an award winner," said Buck who also served as Chamber of Commerce executive director and won the "Mr. Tri-Tip" contest in 1997, the last time the newspaper sponsored the male beauty contest named after the meaty, juicy local barbecue beef specialty before feminists from University of California Santa Barbara followed Paige to church and shamed her in front of her Sunday Bible School class by distributing pictures of Mr. Tri-Tip and Paige dancing on the Elks bar with Paige wearing nothing but her favorite baby blue hair-on-hide rodeo chaps

Paige belched and blushed—a result more of alcohol intake than modesty.

"You're on the state journalism award committee," Steward

said. "Tell your carpetbagger muckraker newsman the fix is in and if he's a good boy you'll get him a first-place column writing award."

"I'll tell Mr. Zarate that we expect one column a week about Delgado's success story," Paige said. "How all of Santa Maria supports him in his bid for the governor's office. How we always report good news when we see it and in Santa Maria there is no such thing as bad news. Not when we're living in paradise."

Buck said, "You're not running anything else in our paper about those psycho killings, are you? Sudden death is bad for tourists and the wine business. Make people think they can get butchered in a wine tasting room or mutilated in a motel swimming pool. Massacres kill a vacation mood real quick."

Paige cooed like an untamed pigeon nestled under a freeway bridge.

"You know me better than that, cowboy."

Slowly twisting his torso her way, Mr. Tri-Tip flexed his chest and tightened his abdomen muscles, passing gas in the process.

"You might make rodeo queen after all, darling."

OF COURSE SHE LOVED WALLY

MIRIAM disappeared on prom night in 1990 with graduation right around the corner. Nobody who knew her whereabouts would say where she went.

When Wally realized for sure she stood him up, he went home, sat on his bed for hours in his cheap, rented tux that made him look like Temptations lead singer David Ruffin on the Steel Pier in Atlantic City in 1966, listening to records he played on the little plastic record player his mom picked up for him at a yard sale for his sixteenth birthday.

An all A-student, Miriam was Wally's only ever girlfriend even if she wouldn't let him pick her up at her house for a date or stop by to walk with her to school. The prom was supposed to be the biggest night ever for each 17 year old.

"I'll meet you there," Miriam said.

Now here he was on that very special prom night, smelling of Ice Blue Aqua Velva aftershave, alone in his room with a fresh orchid corsage in the refrigerator that he bought on sale a week before the dance from the woman who sold flowers on the corner and seemed truly happy for him when he told her in juvenile Spanish that he was in love.

Miriam also sat alone, drained of emotion. Earlier that day, Miriam's mother found the pregnancy test results in Miriam's purse. The abortion Miriam had maturely planned with the counselors at the women's center was now completely out of the question.

More than five billion boys and girls took their first breaths that year, including Wallace, whose daddy had no idea he was born.

Miriam's parents ordered her not to ever tell weird Wally. Miriam did as she was told. She would give birth in Los Angeles and never speak to the father again. Mom and dad kept her on the shortest leash money could buy, renting an apartment 55 miles north in Lompoc for the new single mother and child. Dad had friends at Vandenberg Air Force Base and at the federal prison there. If he had any say in the matter, nobody would touch his irresponsible daughter again. Dad co-signed a used car loan and handled expenses until she got on her feet—far enough away from Santa Barbara that she and "it" would likely never cross paths again.

Shamed and wracked with guilt, Miriam burrowed as deeply into herself as she could. Had mom not busted her and dad forced the psychiatric treatment for schizophrenia and the hospitalization and all the rest of the so-called care for her now increasing manic depression, Miriam might have been afraid to tell Wally anyway. Abortion or no abortion, she was a woman destined to live on her own.

Of course she loved Wally, but started to forget about him when the manager at Goodies supermarket accepted her application and she told her new supervisor her goal in life was to work in a "retail grocery management position." The 50-year-old manager told her she had lots of time for advancement which meant working at the market for the rest of her life, just like him. The manager also told Miriam she was hot.

Miriam officially named the baby after her father, but from day one always called the boy Wallace. After that first year in Lompoc she never saw her parents again. After that she never said her father's name out loud again either. She told her neighbor she named her baby after George Wallace, the late right wing former governor of Alabama, who was related through marriage, which, of course, was a lie.

Miriam slid off her meds and kept slipping.

Every now and then she caught herself wondering how Wally handled prom night when she thought she heard his voice at the door downstairs but put her hands over her ears to keep from hallucinating—a scary phenomenon she and Wally shared. Voices spoke to them both, creating one big unhappy family.

Wally went looking for her that night and knocked on the door of her house. Holding her corsage, wearing his tux, Wally tried to act grown up.

"Is Miriam home?" he asked when her father answered.

"Show your face here again I'll call the police, you demented freak," the man said. "I'm a music industry lawyer. I know rock stars. I'll ruin you."

Wally tried to be brave.

"Miriam is my date and we're going to the prom together, sir," he said.

The man slammed the door. Wally stood facing the brass knocker for a full two minutes, then turned and left, never returning or calling again. He never tried to find Miriam. He refused to talk to his mother about what happened and she knew enough to respect his dejected solitude. Mary Jane left her boy alone. Miriam must have decided he really wasn't for her, Wally thought. So what else was new? Did anybody think Wally was for them?

Miriam never got better. Miriam never got happy. Psychosis enveloped her. Loneliness, bitterness, fear and hatred festered in her heart, sucking all the love from her life, turning her brain into a soft mental swamp where peace of mind sunk to the bottom, anchored in the quicksand of her pain.

Ten years later one of Miriam's co-workers at Goodies said her brother told her the Jews owned everything and that's why they never got raises or better benefits at the supermarket. The Jews ran the insurance companies and even the hospitals. Jews hated California and women and groceries and everybody who wasn't a Jew.

The explanation seemed so rational to Miriam, so simple.

Jews.

Knowing who to blame for everything made Miriam feel better.

One morning when the store opened and the police showed up, Miriam saw that burglars had trashed the bakery. Overnight, vandals smeared the floor, the walls and even hit the ceiling with plump dripping chocolate éclairs and mashed banana custard cakes.

The looters smashed apple pies and trampled into the carpet glazed doughnuts, crumpets and every turnover imaginable.

"Who would do such a thing?" another co-worker asked Miriam.

"Niggers," Miriam said.

Miriam's manager didn't know what to say when the black co-worker reported Miriam.

"What are you saying? Do you know what you're saying? Why did you say that? What is wrong with you?" the manager asked Miriam.

"Niggers are worse than Jews and a hundred times worse than Mexicans," Miriam said. "That's why they don't get married. Even they know what such mutated coupling will produce."

"We will not provide you with a reference," the biracial human resources officer said.

"I always thought you were a Jew," Miriam said. "Bet you date niggers."

At night Miriam told little Wallace what she called "human interest stories" when she tucked him into bed. Listening attentively, he blinked wide-eyed, expressionless. But he listened. As he grew older, skinhead summer camp complemented his political indoctrination as well as his physical development. He made up and told his own human interest stories, bringing sissy boy fags and raghead Muslims into the narrative. Miriam beamed, so very proud of her son even when her condition worsened and she tossed a cocktail of pills into her glass of iced tea as she watched the singing and dancing shows on cable TV.

One night when Wallace was 16, Miriam saw a shadow move past the living room window, maybe a bat or just the movement of the trees in the evening breeze.

"Terrorists," she said. "Shhhh."

Wallace grabbed the pump action riot shotgun from where it leaned against the wall in the corner, cocked it with a one-hand up-and-down motion, and took aim at the dog and cat patterned curtains his mother bought at the thrift store because she loved animals.

"Shoot," Miriam said.

The blast blew out the window and brought police to the house in two minutes.

"Prowler," Wallace said. "With a gun."

"Wearing a James Brown T-shirt," Miriam said.

Thanking mother and son for their neighborhood vigilance and concern for law and order, the two white uniformed cops left the scene of no crime.

"My hero," Miriam said.

Wallace slung his arm around his mother's shoulders and pulled her close.

Another shotgun blast erupted about nine the next morning. Sliding out of bed, Wallace walked calmly downstairs and stood over Miriam's body wearing only white underwear briefs. One minute later Wallace called 911.

"My mother just killed herself with my shotgun," he said. "I'd prefer if only Caucasian officers respond, if you don't mind."

Wallace opened a bottle of German lager, filled and drained a pilsner glass, and waited for the police and coroner to arrive. While he waited he listened to Third Reich marching music on the CD player and opened two more beers.

That morning he never felt more alive.

A MAN OF THE BULLSHIT

THE roar of the crowd took Wally by surprise, sounding like a packed soccer stadium celebrating a surprise goal. Wally heard the cheering before he saw the people gathered by the hundreds in the large strawberry field among row after row of healthy plants bearing ripe, fat, red berries.

Driving back from Guadalupe Beach, a deserted stop on his itinerary he had mapped out before beginning his adventure, Wally wasn't sure what to think. Police stopped traffic and rerouted cars coming toward Santa Maria. Instead of turning left and driving past the vendor selling oranges from his truck at the intersection, Wally pulled over and parked. The bullhorn echoed off tall tan dunes and soft green hills in the distance.

"This is where it started then," the well-dressed man with the bullhorn shouted. "This is where it starts again today."

Rowdy cheers resonated even at a distance, lifting above the sound of live trumpet music. Walking toward the assembly, Wally smelled the strong aroma of strawberries.

Most of the people holding political campaign signs were white. A handful of campaign workers seemed light brown-skinned and wore dress shirts with the occasional dark necktie. Female Oaxacan farmworkers, short and young, stood in a group off to the side. None of them held signs. With their heads and faces wrapped to their eyes in scarves to keep dust from their lungs, they wore baseball caps under hoodies and waited to go back to work.

Each farmworker lost money as each second ticked off the clock. Their supervisors had ordered them to assemble for effect, to make the point that Carlos Delgado was one of them even though he wasn't.

Wally walked closer to the rally as a television crew ran past him, late but hopefully not late enough to miss the big news production, the drama that would make the "film at eleven" that boring local news reporters made such a big deal about in their boring local stories.

"Come to me," Delgado said to the people. "Come to me."

Dropping the bullhorn, he slowly lowered himself to one knee. Blessing himself with his right hand, the crowd followed suit, touching their foreheads for the father, their chests for the son and their left and right shoulders for the Holy Ghost.

Wally stood away from the crowd nearest the workers.

Dropping to both knees now, Delgado bowed his head low then lower, bending at the waist so his nose touched the ground. In several long, dramatic sniffs, he inhaled the earthy smell of the soil, the aroma and essence of his bogus, yet well-orchestrated, political identity.

"Ahhh," Delgado said. "Perfume."

The crowd laughed.

"A new women's perfume line sounds good to me, governor," Paige Pennington said. "A partner for your male aftershave."

Delgado smiled but his eyes grew watery, welling up with well-rehearsed emotion as he recited his next line.

"I am a man of the land," he said.

"You are a man of the bullshit," Syrah said.

Laughing unexpectedly and loudly enough to draw attention to himself, Wally spoke softly, talking to himself.

"Knock it off, Syrah," he said under his breath. "You'll get us in trouble."

Delgado snapped his head in Wally's direction as the executive protection team sensed the hiccup in the well-scripted proceedings and closed in. The strawberry pickers drifted into minimal shade created by the flatbed truck flush with "Vote Delgado" posters and occupied by a 10-man mariachi band in braided red and silver suits.

Confusion reigned when a second voice on a second bullhorn

boomed even louder than Delgado's sharp tones.

"Sí, se puede," a man shouted. "Yes, we can."

This lanky white man in the black uniform of a Roman Catholic priest made his way from the road to the center of the field. With his white clerical collar open and askew, he wore Army jungle boots and humped the land with the practiced gait of a platoon leader. An all-around point man, the priest knew trouble when he saw it and how to deal with chaos when it arrived.

Delgado sensed what was coming—a bad scene he wanted to avoid—especially in front of the news media. The priest immediately saw through his charade. Delgado nodded to his video crew and tried to stay on script. Reaching for a single strawberry, he plucked the fruit from the ground. Rising as promised the night before, he raised the strawberry skyward.

"To you, my precious mother, and you, sainted father of mine," he said. "Like before, when we worked these fields together."

"That's the first goddamn strawberry you ever picked in your life," the priest said. "I've picked more strawberries in a morning to use for communion in the fields with the farmworkers than you will ever pick in your lifetime of deceit."

"Give 'em hell, Padre," Jesús Zarate yelled from the sidelines.

Publisher Paige Pennington gasped, pointing at Jesús.

"You are fired," she said.

"No, señora, liberated," he said.

Perceiving the priest as a great man, Wally wanted to give 'em hell, too. The farmer was no good. Sick as he was, Wally always tried to depend on common sense. Good versus evil, humanity's time-honored tradition of standing against inhumanity, resolving conflict that needed fixed—usually by somebody else, unfortunately—usually made sense. But Wally was always too afraid to get involved.

Walking to the warrior priest who took his stand in muddy combat boots, Wally extended his hand.

"I'm Wally."

"Padre Fresa," the priest said. "Father Strawberry."

"Far out," Wally said.

"Vamonos, "Delgado said. "Let's get out of here."

When the day ended a sleek beast stood alone on a towering nearby sand dune. Watching over the struggle, smelling the sour scent of the human condition, the Magic Coyote turned and ran toward the sun.

I JUST WANT TO SLEEP

"JESUS Christ, the guy's a newspaperman," Wallace said.

"No, it's Jesús Zarate and yes, he's a newspaper columnist who saved us a shit load of trouble," Rose said. "Who reads the paper anymore, anyway?"

"Can we just get off this merry-go-round?" Wallace said

"We just got on," Rose said.

Green neon flashes from the "no vacancy" sign lit Rose's face in the darkened room. Wallace drank warm beer he bought earlier at a package store down the street where he parked his no-shine flat black customized scooter rather than have somebody spot it in the Sea Urchin parking lot.

Drunk, he and Rose felt bad when they should have felt good. Neither had enjoyed such a nice day in a long time. Surfing, eating fish tacos, walking back from Zip's together in the gentle sea breeze. Wallace hadn't punched anybody. Rose hadn't pulled her gun.

"Jesús says a corkscrew killer is on the loose," Wallace said. "Popping eyeballs like wine corks—like we don't have enough problems."

"That's got nothing to do with us, Wallace," Rose said. "I just want to sleep."

Wallace had been feeling the same for too long. Sleep forever. Step in front of the crazy train. He never talked with anybody about feeling so bad he wanted to check out. He never wanted to think about it himself. But when the urge came, he shivered. And the urge was coming more and more lately. His mother never talked about it either. But he felt too close for comfort.

89

"You ever think about ending it?" he asked Rose.

"Ending what?"

"Your life."

"Sure," she said.

Starting to cry, she reached for the beach bag. Removing the gun, she placed it on the dresser by the TV.

"You?"

"When I got back from Afghanistan the last time. When I left Iraq the first time. When I hooked up with the Crushers. But the club saved my life."

"Saved it for what?"

"For you?"

"There's no future for me, you or us, Wallace. You think I'm going to live my life riding behind you in the bitch seat with you calling me your old lady? Think again."

Wallace reached into the paper bag and pulled out two warm cans of Bud. Handing one to Rose he started to tremble. The question had to be asked.

"You want to check out together?" he asked.

Wallace didn't mean from the Sea Urchin. He finally had a partner, a real partner who cared for him and for whom he cared. They could wrap it up on a high note. End it all together. Rose even had a gun.

Twenty minutes passed without a word. Drinking the last of the beer, they took slow sips and shared quick glances. Wallace walked to the dresser, picked up the nine, and made sure a round was racked into the chamber.

"I'm going to put the gun here on the dresser," he said. "We're going to go to sleep. If I wake up and decide to die, I get out of bed, get the gun and shoot you in the head. Then I shoot myself."

Rose could hear her pulse banging in her ears.

"If I wake up and want to die," she said. "I get out of bed, walk to the dresser, pick up the gun and shoot you in the head. Then I shoot myself."

A cricket chirped in a bush outside the window.

"Good night, Wallace."

"Good night, Rose."

YOU BELIEVE IN BUDDHA?

"THANKS for the lift, Wally."

"You're welcome, Father."

"As a reciprocal gesture of your kindness, I'm inviting you to Lupe's eighth birthday party. I baptized her. She's a wonderful child. You Catholic, Wally?"

Wally did not know how to answer.

"My mother told me I was a child of the universe."

Father Fresa nodded, recognizing Wally as a serious middle-aged thinker—sincerely introspective and somewhat lost. The priest wanted to protect and respect his feelings.

"Your mother was right, buddy. It's okay not to be Catholic, Wally. I'm not Catholic either."

Looking puzzled, Wally's face gave him away. Picking up on the mood, Father Fresa sensed many questions as Wally's tight white knuckles gripped the steering wheel.

"You heard of a lapsed Catholic? I'm a collapsed Catholic. Packed it in the same day I threw my medal over the fence at the White House a long, long time ago."

"But you're still a priest?"

"On my terms. On God's terms. Not the Pope's terms or the cardinal's terms or the bishop's terms. My goddamn terms. Life's terms. Universal terms, Wally. We are all children of the universe."

Wally felt good listening to the priest, like he mattered, like he didn't need anybody's approval to be who he was or feel good about the cosmos and the sweet mysteries of life.

"You give communion to the workers in the fields?"

"Only the workers," the priest said. "True children of the land, of God or Buddha or Santa Muerte, the Mexican death saint."

"You believe in Buddha?" Wally asked.

"I believe in everybody, man."

"What kind of medal did you throw over the fence?"

"My Medal of Honor."

Trying to gauge the priest's age, Wally guessed maybe 74, a strong, healthy, rugged 74. White stubble poked through the skin of his cheeks even though the priest likely had shaved that morning. Reddish freckles dotted the tops of his hands. A lock of soft white hair across his eyebrow then swept back with the same across-the-forehead motion John and Bobby Kennedy used. The thighs of the priest's black pants, shiny from too much wear and tear, matched the elbows of his coat that showed fraying around the edges. The once heavily starched white collar had yellowed at the bottom and seemed permanently sweat-stained at the top.

"Vietnam?" Wally said.

"Vietnam."

"I was too young to go," Wally said.

"So was I."

On both sides of the van some of the best black soil in the world flashed by in a blur. Other than strawberries, the dark, loamy fields produced broccoli, cauliflower, lettuce, celery and other vegetables. Farmers planted more and more blueberries, as well.

"When I see the Mexicans," the priest said. "I see the Irish. Picking slate and working as breaker boy child laborers in Pennsylvania hard coal country. I see the Vietnamese working in rice paddies. I see good, decent people getting ripped off, getting sick and hurt. Asking for nothing and getting less."

A dusty crossroads loomed in the distance.

"Almost there," the priest said.

"I don't speak Spanish," Wally said.

"That'll make it even," the priest said. "Lupe's parents and friends don't speak English."

Motioning to a small West Main Street store with cracked orange plaster and a paint-chipped coin-operated rocking horse by the door, the priest asked Wally to pull over.

"I'll be right back," he said.

When he returned, he carried a paper grocery sack bulging with cellophane bags loaded with bright Mexican candy.

"Órale," the priest said. "Let's go."

About a dozen children gathered excitedly around the van as Wally pulled to the curb. Squealing, they ran in circles when the priest stepped from the passenger seat making a face and holding out his hands like a monster.

"Yo soy Cucuy! El Cucuy Mexicano! El Cucuy Mexicano!" he said in a deep, ominous voice so fake it wouldn't scare anybody but the smallest child. "I am Cooo- cuey! The boogeyman. The Mexican boogeyman."

Shrieking boys and girls scattered up and down the dirt yard laughing so hard some fell or started to cough or put their hands over their eyes. The bravest ran to the priest, grabbing his pants leg before running away, making you-can't-catch-me faces before bolting behind bushes and trees.

Wally never saw anything like this joyous scene. As instructed, he brought the bulging paper sack to the priest who threw it high into the air. When the cellophane bags he already opened hit the concrete, they burst like mini piñatas, showering red, green, purple, blue and yellow wrapped Mexican candies—sweet, fruity, salty, sour, spicy treats—all over the sidewalk. Like happy piranhas on a meaty soup bone, the children swooped and scooped up as much as they could carry. One boy with ink black hair got so excited he opened two different candies at the same time and stuffed them both into his mouth.

"Mission accomplished," Father Fresa said.

Lupe spotted him through the open door from where she stood by the kitchen table upon which her moist two flavor, three milks—tres leches—birthday cake sat in the center.

"Today is my birthday, Father," she said.

Bending to hug the child, the priest stood and shook hands all around. Men and women fresh from the fields gathered around the tall man dressed in the uniform of their faith, smiling shyly and speaking deferentially in low voices.

"Este es mi amigo, Wally," the priest said.

"Hi Wally," Lupe said. "This is my mother and father."

"Mucho gusto," said her father.

"Mucho gusto," said her mother.

Except to order food on the rare occasion he felt brave enough to go into a real Mexican restaurant, Wally never used Spanish. He thought these words meant "pleased to meet you," but wasn't sure.

"Much gusto to you, as well," Wally said.

Affection filled the room that pulsed with corrido music from the radio and smelled of freshly cut limes, beans boiling in a pot and hand-pressed tortillas hot from the frying pan. Somebody dug into a cooler loaded with ice and handed Wally a cold can of Tecate. Somebody fixed him a plate and pointed to the dish of homemade salsa.

"Picante," a woman said.

Piled high, the spicy green salsa, boiled beans, tortillas and Mexican beer smelled and looked better than any meal Wally could remember.

"Muchas gracias," he said.

For a moment Wally believed with all his heart that he was Mexican.

As the evening picked up and wore on, people treated Wally as one of their own, like he belonged and didn't have to do anything to please anyone except respect those who respected him—which seemed to him to be everybody at the party.

Father Fresa lit into dancing a foot stomping regional dance from Morelia, Michoacan, with Lupe's aunt in the kitchen. As the dance party moved to the adjacent living room the floor shook. Lamps moved on tables. Pictures rattled on the walls. The dance reminded Wally of the Bristol Stomp he saw in reruns of American Bandstand he watched with his mother before she died.

When all eyes turned his way, when little Lupe ran to his side and said, "C'mon, Wally, dance," Wally didn't know what to do but dance.

Putting his hands on his hips, he leaned in and shuffled twice with his left foot and twice with his right foot, almost stumbling, but staying upright in an awkward series of steps. Watching Lupe who made the dance look so easy and fluid and fun, he tried his best to follow her lead. People grinned and moved back, making way to give Wally room. And dance he did, somehow picking up the rhythm, the cadence of the music and the motion, like he was settling into a supernatural structure that felt like dancing on clouds. People started clapping as Wally made his final turns and the song on the radio ended. Facing Lupe, Wally bowed. In response she curtsied. Father Fresa rushed over with another cold Tecate and handed the can to Wally.

"You're a natural, señor," he said.

"Gracias, padre," Wally said.

YOU AN ADDICT?

"GOOD morning, Wallace."
   "Good morning, Rose."

Breakfast aromas smelled great—fried eggs, peppers, onions and potatoes drifting in the open window from the street. The gun remained untouched on the dresser. Wallace slid out of bed, walked to the open window, and looked across the tree tops to the thin blue strip of ocean he could see in the distance. Rose slid out the other side and casually put the gun back in her beach bag.

"I'm starving," Wallace said.

"I could eat," Rose said.

"You a big eater?" Wallace asked.

"No."

Rose seemed sad yet agitated.

"We're starting all over today, right?"

"First day and all that horseshit," Wallace said.

"So, I've got to level with you."

"So, level."

"I'm running low on Hydrocodone and Oxycodone."

"You have a prescription?"

"No."

"You an addict?"

"Yes."

"So we're screwed and I don't mean corkscrewed."

"Excuse me?"

"It never stops, does it?" Wallace said. "We can't start fresh, can we? What do you say we just end it now?"

Rose looked startled. **97**

"Not like that. Not like we talked about last night. End it like you go left and I'll go right."

"Like you don't have your own problems? I'm not the one with voices in my head. The psycho combat vet. And I'm not the former president of a national outlaw motorcycle gang who's on the run for the rest of his life."

"The same bad boys looking for me are looking for you."

"So we're both fucked."

Wallace lit a cigarette.

"You're not allowed to smoke in this room. You really ought to think about quitting," Rose said.

"You don't smoke?"

"No. It's a filthy habit that will kill you."

"Listen to little Miss Painkiller lecturing me about health and fitness."

"You need your meds and won't take them. I don't need the pills and eat them like gummy worms. For what it's worth, I want to stop."

Staring hard at Rose, Wallace butted his cigarette into the palm of his hand, not flinching at the little bit of pain from the red hot ash. Wallace had felt much worse.

JUST SIT

Back on the beach at Guadalupe, Wally sat on the sand cross-legged, watching waves roll in and waves roll out. Zazen felt good for the soul he told the priest at the birthday party. To his surprise the priest agreed and said he planned to start sitting zazen himself.

On this day Wally just sat listening to the wind and the ocean, feeling the sea spray on his face. Ten minutes earlier a dolphin surfaced and rode one of the swells almost all the way to shore before rolling and turning back into the water. A minute later the sleek mammal surfaced again and rode another wave. Wally wondered if he saw one or two dolphins, maybe a couple. Either way, these beautiful animals were free and seemingly having fun as part of the ocean, helping maintain life on this glorious planet that Wally shared with these awesome creatures and all other living species.

Looking left and right, Wally saw no one. Two Filipino fishermen had packed up their long casting poles and left. A young Mexican couple folded their bright blanket, tidied up from their picnic, and disappeared over cascading sand dunes that defined this beach as unique.

Primitively beautiful, the government refused to allow private developers to build on this stretch of sand and sea that displayed California holy land as far as you could see. Hollywood occasionally shot movies and car commercials there. Cecil B. DeMille in 1923 chose carefully and filmed the "The Commandments" in these flowing mountainous dunes.

With a prophet's tone Father Fresa told Wally that Guadalupe held wisdom for those willing to accept the harsh reality of their lives. That night after the party Wally drove the half hour back to the two-lane entrance with a wooden guard shack and a "closed" sign on the gate.

Living dangerously, Wally parked the van along the road, packed his canvas rucksack with a plastic container of rice and beans slathered with hot salsa verde sauce, a few cans of Tecate and a piece of Lupe's birthday cake wrapped in a napkin, and started his hike up the road through the dunes. His flashlight beam danced beneath the moonlight. Wally saw silhouettes of coyotes running across the dune horizon and heard them howl in greeting. Wally howled back. Feeling alive and spiritual, Wally hiked the mile or so past the river that flowed into the sea and through magnificent sand hills to the beach.

Wally found a spot and sat quietly. Ocean waves whispered "enlightenment" in his ears. Coyotes chanted wild hymns and the hidden movie set of buried pyramids held secrets of yesterday Wally swore he could feel vibrate beneath his bottom. Today is what matters Wally thought. Tomorrow might never come. Stars danced across the sky and in the distance a boat's light drifted across the horizon powered by music in Wally's head.

"Howling at the coyotes, Wally," Syrah said. "Really?"

Knocking Wally off his briefly confident psychedelic mental balance beam, Syrah's tone signaled some serious annoyance.

"Where's your bamboo flute, Wally?"

Wally stuttered.

"I'm happy for right now," he said. "Right now I'm not sad about my mother, about failing all my life, about the prom or about bad people who seem to be everywhere."

"You're not sad about bad people, Wally? The bad people you wiped out? You're not sad about those three orbs you popped like the maraschino cherry you served in a wine glass to that spoiled little lady at the winery?"

"That wasn't my fault. The manager said she'd fire me if I didn't serve Margot another glass of wine. I mean sparkling water."

"With a cherry."

"I had to."

"You could have refused."

"You could have saved her Poppy's life by not pushing me."

"You killed him, Wally."

No, you killed him."

"You."

"No, you."

Wally felt his gray matter start to boil.

"We killed him, Wally," Syrah said. "Poppy deserved to croak."

Adjusting his sitting position, Wally half closed his eyes and tried to ignore Syrah's voice. She was right, always right. And he trusted her guidance. Inhaling deeply, he slowly exhaled, trying to sense every moment and every moment between moments. His head returned to feeling nice inside. The mind monkeys slowed down. They needed rest as well.

The more zazen Wally did, the less Syrah appeared. Her absence gave him hope, helping him feel he was right all along, that he didn't need the medication. Ocean breeze and zazen ease went together like peanut butter and strawberry preserves. Wally suddenly wanted to go swimming but was afraid of jelly fish.

Without warning an alarm went off like a nuclear power plant siren in his head, radiating in his brain when Syrah started screaming. Wally knew no escape. Wally prepared for trouble.

"Intruder at 10 o'clock," Syrah howled. "Intruder at 10 o'clock."

Wally stiffened.

Opening his eyes he saw the figure move up the beach from the Point Sal side. Dressed in black, wearing what looked like a long pleated skirt, Jesús walked awhile and jogged awhile and walked and jogged again. Extending his right arm, he leaned to touch the sand with his little finger, rolled up the arm and over the shoulder. Coming to his feet he walked without breaking stride, jogged and rolled up his left arm. This alternating rolling brought him closer and closer to Wally, who just sat quietly, doing nothing. Jesús planned to roll on by but Wally spoke when he got close.

"Aikido," Wally said, pointing at him.

"Zazen," Jesús said, pointing at Wally.

They laughed.

"Zen and aikido complement each other," Wally said.

"You practice?" Jesús asked.

"No, but I read. You sit?" Wally asked.

"Yes."

"Aikido is moving Zen," Jesús said. "You watch the waves, right?"

Wally nodded.

"See how they come in and break, still washing up on the beach yet beginning to recede at almost the same time?"

Wally nodded.

"Like a circle. Sacred Zen circles signal the beginning and the end. But there is no beginning. There is no end. Everything is connected. Everything is impermanent."

"Everything is everything," Wally said.

"Yeah," Jesús said. "Everything is everything."

Waves broke softly on the sand.

"Maybe I'll see you in the dojo," Jesús said. "Henry's House of Aiki."

"Maybe you will," Wally said.

"I saw you yesterday at the Delgado rally. You left with the priest," Jesús said.

"I saw you, as well," Wally said.

"Good ki," Jesús said.

"Karma," Wally said.

As Jesús walked away he thought of the Buddhism he didn't really understand but tried to practice anyway. Spiritual mystery attracted him, such as directions from Zen masters to "kill the Buddha" or "die on your cushion." Jesús promised himself that one day he would understand the meaning of those words.

Wally watched Jesús walk away until he disappeared at the far end of the beach. Wally stood and picked up a long piece of drift wood that washed up on the beach. Looking like a monk with a walking stick, Wally slowly turned a complete circle, using the stick to carve in one fluid motion in the wet sand a perfect sacred Zen circle the Japanese call enso. In seconds the next wave arrived to erase his work. Thrilled, Wally drew another enso and another and another after that.

"You hear them, Wally?" Syrah screamed. "You hear the bongos? You really should be hearing bongos, Wally."

All Wally heard was the soothing sound of satori massaging a song of friendship into the tender nerve centers of his psyche. Wally vowed to do some aikido in the future—learn the way of peace and harmony. Maybe take a yoga class, too. Wally liked walking the soft path because the walk did him good.

A walk on the soft path does everybody good.

MEXICAN GANG HIT

T

"SIGNS of a struggle," Detective Danny Gagliardi said. "Don't anybody touch anything until forensics gets here."

The imitation white pearl handle of a foot-long butcher knife protruded from the priest's chest, marking a dark crimson stain in the center of the black shirt. Blood puddled around the body. Open at the neck, the priest's white collar showed blood spatter. Black sport coat, black pants, black socks and black shoes rounded out his outfit for dying.

"Mexican gang hit," Gagliardi said. "Los Matadores. No doubt in my mind. The priest was giving the people too much hope. The gang doesn't want them to have hope. Detracts from their power."

The detective lied. Padding the numbers and blaming everything bad on the Mexicans was the name of the game in Santa Maria. A proud Swiss Italian—meaning Tyrolian heritage and a dairy farming background—Gagliardi hated Mexicans even though he tried not to show it through overt racism. Ashamed of the farmworkers' honor and hard work in Santa Maria, he wanted a promotion so much he attended community college classes where he learned little.

On the payroll and working security at night for Delgado, patrolling the empty warehouses for a few bucks under the table, driving the field dictator in his new luxury pickup, making sure Delgado's wife didn't catch him with his girlfriends, Gagliardi expected a job as head of the state security detail when Delgado won the governor's job.

Of course, he knew who killed the priest and why. The priest did give the people hope but it wasn't the Chicano gang-bangers who felt threatened. Delgado and his crew felt threatened—including Detective Gagliardi.

The final struggle occurred when Gagliardi, wielding a pool cue, caught the priest on top of his head in the darkness behind the homeless shelter, knocking him to his knees but not knocking him out. As the big man struggled to get to his feet, this same detective wearing shades, a black cowboy hat and a black bandana across his mouth and nose, plunged the butcher knife into his chest. The weapon originated in the SMPD evidence locker and had been used in an unsolved murder more than thirty years ago. About 50 witnesses knew who killed that man in the public park, but he was Mexican and his killer was Mexican and the cops, including Gagliardi, didn't care enough to do anything about it.

The bad cop's cell phone rang.

"We'll call a press conference tomorrow at nine in the strawberry field to announce a reward for any information leading to the arrest and conviction of the gang members who murdered the priest," Delgado said.

"How much?" Gagliardi asked.

"Five thousand dollars."

"Too much."

"Like somebody's going to collect? You thinking of turning yourself in?" Delgado said.

"When are you holding your next fundraiser?"

"As soon as they bury this puta priest. Right after his funeral. And I mean right after. We pay for the community wake. Beer, food, music, speeches. Tell the people we will now help them as he helped them. We will take up his causes and protect them. The priest would understand and support my campaign."

"Nobody's going to buy that, Mr. Delgado."

"They have no choice."

"Why is that?"

"I always win. They always lose."

Driving back into town from Guadalupe, looking to find his new priest friend, Wally again saw flashing lights—this time farther up the road to Santa Maria at the second crossroads where he and Father Fresa had stopped for candy. Pulling to the side of the road, he asked a uniformed officer what had happened.

"Please move along," the portly white cop said.

Wally parked the van beside the statue of a big bull at a small market. Word spread among the field workers who gathered in the small shopping center of stores that sold clothing and beer and other day-to-day needs to farmworkers and their families. The notorious pool hall was closed so young men gathered in the parking lot, kept at bay by yellow police tape. Word leaked quickly that somebody murdered Father Fresa. Anger spread. Lupe's aunt, with whom the holy priest had danced just the day before, stood on the sidewalk by a traditional Mexican seafood restaurant. Wally saw her crying, walked to her side and spoke his soft halting Spanish.

"Buenas tardes, señora," Wally said.

All the woman could do was cry.

"Father Fresa," she said.

"Sí," Wally said.

"Father Fresa está muerto."

Despite his lack of language, Wally knew.

Salty tears burned into his eyes. The smells of lunch fajitas, grilled tacos and fresh ceviche with cilantro, cucumber, fresh lime and fat shrimp filled the air. A car radio pounded out a ranchero tune. A teenager threw a Negra Modelo bottle that smashed near the boots of a young man who kicked the brown pieces of glass beneath the tires of a parked and dented used Chevy pickup truck.

Wally heard bongos.

BUNCHES OF PUNCHES

Jesús Zarate never forgot where he came from. Too much was riding on remembering.

"Take the guilty plea and cop to manslaughter," the public defender said that day so long ago. "The judge will go easy."

"Guilty," Jesús said.

"Ten years," the judge said.

"Damn, homes," said the lawyer. "Man hit you with a deuce. Sorry about that."

Jesús' crash and burn started at 4 a.m. in late summer in El Diablo, the most popular Mexican nightclub in Santa Maria. After inhaling four small spoonsful of cocaine, 8 little pills of white cross speed, five beers and two White Russians, Jesús and his bloodstream seethed. Standing alone at the bar, he waited for the man to leave.

Earlier in the evening the man had called Jesús a "cocksucker" and "motherfucker." A simple misunderstanding, with insults real or imagined, can lead to destruction. Unbridled violence is sometimes a matter of untamed honor. Jesús should have walked away from the silly argument about who bumped into whom, but chose to avenge the abstract insult to his mother.

When the man left, Jesús followed. In the parking lot Jesús tapped him on the shoulder. When the man turned, he caught a vicious open-hander, meaning to remedy the slight without causing real harm, more to make a point than to injure. The man seemed stunned, infuriated by the slap. He chose to take the confrontation to a higher level.

"I have something in my pocket you are not man enough for me to use it on," the man said. "So I'm going to knock you down and let you get up then knock you down again. I'll show how a hard man fights, a real Mexican Mafia man."

Jesús thought his opponent was talking about a gun. Now he was talking about an endless beating at the hands of the Mexican Mafia. Who was this guy, Chuck Norris? Jesús wondered if the metal taste in his mouth was adrenaline, fear or some heavy protection from his patron saint, Jesús Malverde. As soon as the man moved, more than a little bit of madness blasted off. Always a slugger, Jesús pumped bunches of punches, banging both arms up and down like iron pistons driving at 6,000 rpm full throttle into the man's face.

Jesús came to his senses on his knees, straddling the man and still pounding with his left fist. As the man's face turned a deeper shade of blue, fresh blood up to Jesús' elbows glistened in the overhead parking lot lights. A police car pulled in, the cops got out and heard Jesús screaming into the empty face of death, "I told you to leave me alone."

Some startled gangbanger in a car turned up the volume on a Chalino narcocorrido song about an AK-47 and the late delivery of a heroin score secured in the body cavity of a corpse.

Somebody screamed in time to the lyrics.

Aiiiiiiiii.

A hard man on the ground, a real Mexican Mafia man, never breathed again.

SYRAH PUSHES ON

Without a mirror or assistance, using the scissors on his Swiss Army knife, Wally cut his already short hair to the scalp as closely as he could. After dipping his head in the ocean, he lathered up his scalp with Gillette Foamy Regular Shaving Cream and shaved his skull with a plastic, disposable Bic Sensitive single blade razor. Nicks, abrasions and a few small cuts would heal. The biggest wound would exist in his heart.

In the aftermath of Father Fresa's murder Wally needed to sacrifice.

Then Wally sat zazen.

"I'm not shaving my head, underarms, legs or crotch," Syrah said. "I need a drink."

Trying to ignore the voice, Wally knew the politician with the bullhorn had something to do with the murder, that Los Matadores had no beef with the priest who had helped some of them and their families whose poverty always escaped the attention of local government leaders. As loco as cholos lived, they respected the priest and would have never hurt, let alone kill, him.

Syrah taunted Wally.

"Who's your candidate for governor, Wally?" she asked. "Want to dance, Wally? You got a medal to throw over the fence at the White House, Wally?"

That last put-down got to him.

"No, no I don't" he said. "But if I did I'd do exactly what Father did. I'd give it back. Father wanted peace, peace of mind for me and you and him and everybody. That's what he wanted. He never killed anybody in that war. He saved 22 wounded men, dragging them to safety and out of the line of fire. He would have saved the Viet Cong, too, if he could have."

"And where did our hero's bravery get him, Wally?"

Wally stared at the shimmering horizon.

"Our hero's bravery got him killed," Wally said.

"Nobody dragged him out of the line of fire, Wally."

"Nobody."

"Nobody pulled him to safety, Wally."

"Nobody."

"When would you like to kill the next governor, Wally?"

Gulls cried long, choking calls from the sky, sailing on soft pockets of wind that carried them gliding overhead, high above mushy cocoa brown sand. There, a lonely aspiring monk sat cross-legged with only his tears and vanquished dreams of harmony to keep him company.

"Si," Syrah said. "You are one bald and crazy gringo."

Wally heard bongos.

GROW A LITTLE WEED

"No drugs," Wallace said.

"No drugs," Rose said.

"You can't lie to me, either," he said. "You have to promise."

"Junkies aren't good at promises."

"No opioids," he said.

"No cigarettes for you."

"Throw the gun off the pier into the ocean," he said.

"Jesus fucking Christ, we got killer Crushers on our ass and you want to go unarmed."

"My knife goes, too."

"You're serious?"

"Last night we were talking about killing ourselves, killing each other. We made it through alive. The only way we'll ever make it together is clean, sober, straight and peaceful."

"Maybe we should throw each other off the pier."

Wallace laughed.

"If we make it to Stinson Beach, up in Marin County, we can plan to go the next step, hide out forever up in the Northern California wilderness. Maybe we can compromise, still drink some beers, some red wine. Smoke a little weed. Grow a little weed, but no hard drugs and no guns."

"No shit?"

"No shit."

Wallace reached for a Lucky. Rose slapped his hand away from the pack.

"Starting now, Wallace?"

"Starting now."

"Can I shoot myself first, before I throw the gun off the pier?"

"That's not funny, Rose."

"Yeah, it is, Wallace. This is maybe the funniest fucking time in my whole life ever."

"Shhhhh. You hear that? Outside the door."

Wallace touched the handle of his knife. Rose reached for her beach bag. They grabbed for the door knob at the same time. Tripping over each other to get outside, they spilled into the walkway outside their motel room.

Rose immediately spotted the pile.

"Who would let their dog shit outside a motel room door?"

Wallace knew better.

"No dog did that," he said.

Rose knew better, too.

"An animal," she said.

"The Animal," he said.

WINE POWER

"REMEMBER the good old days, Wally?"
Syrah kept jabbering.
"C'mon, Wally, snap out of it."

For the second day in a row Wally grieved, sitting cross-legged, alone on Guadalupe Beach. Early morning worked best for him, a good time to clear his head and reflect. But Syrah got up even earlier and was ready to greet him with her own delirious take on daybreak.

"You need a drink, son," she said. "Chardonnay for everybody, Wally?"

Wally's depression flared. Trying to swim clear of angst over his new friend's death, he filled his mind with thoughts about all the Mexican children he had met with Father Fresa, how they embodied beauty, adorable in their unassuming lives, the most beautiful children Wally had ever seen.

Straight black hair cascaded down the backs of little girls so demure and polite that you couldn't help feel their innocence along with little boys with eyes shining so brilliantly that they lit the darkest midnight sky. Loose laughter when they shared their childish happiness sounded more joyful than the most angelic singers in the most magnificent cathedral.

Wally loved children and children loved Wally—except for that one lost little soul who found no favor in him and whose face would haunt him forever. This morning Wally could not get snippy vanilla Margot, the prima donna princess at the winery, out of his mind.

Margot's "Poppy" remained the only "wipeout" that troubled

him. That's what Syrah called the killings—wipeouts, like the surf term. Poppy loomed large in Wally's mind, a recurrent ghost and Wally's first victim, his introduction to mindless murder.

Death for the other three stiffs qualified as well-deserved. Poppy asked for it, too, humiliating Wally, hurting and pushing too far for anybody's good. Wally saw how Poppy abused his little princess, grooming her into a lush at seven, grievous behavior that would grate on God. For that trespass, Poppy's pupil must pop. Pop goes the eyeball.

Getting past the bongos in his head that day at the winery exhausted Wally, who was hearing them play for the very first time. Electric surf music refried his brain. But when Mommy and Margot excused themselves to go to what Margot called "the little girls' powder room," steel guitars kicked in and Wally got down to business.

"Oh, I am so sorry," Wally said to Poppy. "Please allow me to make up for the error of my ways."

Poppy looked at Wally like he was a bug.

"Nothing you do will compensate for your impudence toward Margot."

"I'd like to give you a free case of our finest chardonnay."

Greed flashed in Poppy's eyes.

"Please meet me outside," Wally said.

Poppy was waiting when Wally got there, licking his lips knowing he would get something for nothing, exactly the way he liked living life. Walking together down the grassy hill to the wine cave, Wally strolled through canyon fields of luxuriant grass to a trimmed secluded spot where several 24,000 gallon industrial strength stainless steel fermentation storage units stood. The tanks would soon hold the freshest soon-to-be-bottled chardonnay steeped to perfection. Now they stood empty.

Wally talked a bit about the product. The man knew so little about chard that Wally, with what little wine talk practice he had, impressed Poppy on the way to the much anticipated freebie.

"You will absolutely adore the scent of crème brulee topped by a toasty mango swirl so bright you can light up your life with it,"

Wally said.

"Dazzling," Poppy said.

"But, first, allow me to show you something few chardonnay drinkers ever see," Wally said. "Climb up the ladder and look over the rim of the tank. Tell me what enchanted surprise you see."

Poppy scaled the ladder with the exuberance of the dancing pony he bought Margot for her last birthday. When he got to the top he peered inside. The unfilled tank twinkled so he leaned deeper into the emptiness just in case he missed whatever alchemy revelation he was supposed to notice.

One solid conk on the top of the skull with an empty bottle of citrusy chard that would have gone well with lobster bisque or leek and ham pie accompanied by grilled pineapple sent Poppy swandiving headfirst into the tank.

Landing unconscious on the porous metal drain floor, face forward on the seed screen, Poppy expired almost immediately. Wally tossed the bottle in after him, slammed the lid and made sure to keep the latch unlocked.

"Wine power," said the husky voice of Syrah who controlled his head.

Wally immediately went back to work at the tasting room, pouring more wine, offering less chat.

"Laguna Hills Footwear Designer Missing at Santa Barbara Winery," read the headline in the Sunday Los Angeles Times. The story quoted the winery manager saying she saw Poppy leave the tasting room alone and thought he was returning to the Rolls to wait for his wife and child. Margot told reporters she was sad because Poppy gave her a weekly allowance and with him gone her cash would be delayed. Mommy discreetly called her pool boy on her cell to say he should make no comment and meet her at midnight in the cabana with some herb.

Neither police nor journalists officially interviewed Wally because Wally never mattered.

When workers found the body the next day, fermenting in its own juices, Wally simply told police that the deceased had been a belligerent drunk who likely stole a bottle of their best full-bodied white, with floral notes and a fruitier profile, stumbled drunk to the tank ladder, climbed and fell, breaking his jowly neck in the process. He must have been trying to open the bottle and lost his balance, Wally said, because a corkscrew was stuck in his eye where he obviously had fallen on it during his plunge.

"So sad" Wally said. "His daughter is such a flawless little person."

"Not bad for a beginner, "Syrah said. "The corkscrew was a nice touch."

Behold the future.

"I can see it now," Wally said.

An eye for an eye.

TO LIFE

THE front page banner headline in the Santa Maria Mirror read, "Los Matadores Execute Beloved Priest." The crime shocked the city so badly the paper went ape shit in its coverage.

Throwing the newspaper across the cramped living room of his apartment, Jesús Zarate spoke out loud to himself.

"Too bad they dumped their primo columnist," he said.

City police agreed with candidate Delgado who issued a gubernatorial campaign statement accusing the local gangsters with their Sinaloa cartel connections of killing Father Fresa because they resented him taking the side of "the peasants."

Jesús knew better.

Holding a bottle of Patrón Silver tequila in his lap, he jumped from the couch. Moving quickly to the kitchen, he placed the bottle beside a bowl of limes. Grabbing a paring knife from the dish drainer, he speared a lime and cut the fruit into slices, stacking thin pieces in a brown pottery bowl he remembered his mother using when he was child. Filling a matching earthenware salt shaker, he stood back to admire his work.

Three strong knocks told Jesús his guest had arrived.

"El Maloso," Jesús said when he opened the door. "Buenas tardes."

"Good to see you, El Coyote."

The men embraced.

"Siéntese, por favor," Jesús said.

"What's with the Mexican talk? We're All American good citizens, right?"

"You're the guy everybody still calls El Maloso. The bad guy?"

"Bet nobody calls you Coyote anymore. Remember that night that weightlifter guard screamed like a 5 year old and swore he saw a snarling coyote roaming the block near your cell? Shit, homie, I thought I saw that creature, too. "

Jesús showed his teeth.

"They made the screw take a vacation and see a counselor," he said.

"I know that was you," El Maloso said. "Do the animal spirits still watch your back? Do you still have the ability to change?"

"We see what we want to see," Jesús said.

Teasing was easy. Few men could play with El Maloso. Jesús had earned the right in prison. Filling two shot glasses, Jesús wagged his finger near El Maloso's face, a dangerous move for any man. Jesús would never offer such a vulnerable opening to anyone else.

Sitting across from each other, Jesús and El Maloso lifted their glasses.

"To life," Jesús said.

"To death," said El Maloso.

Licking salt they poured into their hands, they drank smooth raw tequila and sucked sour juice from thick pieces of lime.

"I am happy to see you," El Maloso said. "I thought you were dead."

"I was," Jesús said. "I thought you were dead, too."

"Yeah, I was, too."

"We're both shadows."

"Living in LA is always better when most people can't see you."

Jesús poured two more shots.

"I read your newspaper columns online," El Maloso said.

"Not any more you don't."

"Fired again?"

Jesús shrugged.

"I'm done with the words."

"Now what, compa?"

"My mission is to find my mother," Jesús said. "I believe she's in Culiacan."

"I have a mission," El Maloso said. "Get even with that cabron who disrespected Los Matadores by blaming us for a hit we did not commit. It is bad about the priest. But our revenge is drawn from the disrespect to our familia, not from the death of the priest."

"I understand," said Jesús. "Can I talk you out of the final counterpunch?"

"You know as much about counterpunching as anybody. Payback is always necessary."

Jesús met his eyes and held his gaze.

El Maloso spoke first.

"You saved my life during the riot inside. I only saw the shank when you knocked it from the enforcer's hand. Since then, like it or not, you are Los Matadores. You are my brother."

"The feeling is mutual. You kept the Mexican Mafia at bay when they wanted my head for killing their man," Jesús said.

"So you will not interfere with our plan?"

"No," Jesús said.

"If you need backup when you get to Sinaloa, you will ask for our help?"

"Yes."

One more shot for the road?"

"Sí, un más."

"Viva Jesús Malverde."

"Viva Jesús Malverde."

PRIZE-WINNING CHARDONNAY

WITH sunrise about an hour away Wally shoved his right hand deep into the pocket of his black jeans. Standing by the coin-operated kiddie ride horse outside a small Michoacan ice cream parlor in Santa Maria, he let his mind wander. Next door display lights at the "Delgado for Governor" campaign office flickered in the storefront window.

When Wally was about 4, his mother gently sat him on a similar horse and dropped a dime into the slot. Afraid at first, Wally soon warmed to the gently rocking bucking bronco, squealed and loved every second of the ride.

"More, mommy, more" he said.

Mary Jane put five more dimes in the coin box attached to the ceramic horse's head.

"Mommy's little cowboy," Mary Jane said.

Back then the cast aluminum horse sported a genuine tooled leather saddle adorned with polished silver studs. Bright paint shined from the pony's nose to tail. Today rust crippled the legs. Chipped paint cracked beneath the once proud stallion's eyes. A hole sharp and ragged around the edges gaped in the once powerful belly of this magnificent steed.

Wanting so much to ride once again, Wally held back his tears. Crass laughter and louder cumbia music tore him from his sentimental longing for yesterday.

A drunk and disheveled Delgado parked his yellow Silverado pickup by the curb, leaped from the driver's side, and hurried to open the door for his passenger. Black hair hung in her eyes. Brandishing inch-long blue fingernails imprinted with tiny red hot pepper designs by famous Santa Maria nail artist Sinaloa Lucy, she brushed back her bangs. Sliding smooth tan legs off the seat and carrying a black stiletto pump in each hand, she stepped onto the running board. As the couple had obviously been out all night, Delgado's vaunted Republican family values vanished in the pre-dawn darkness.

Fumbling for the keys to campaign headquarters, Delgado grabbed for whatever part of his date he could reach. Giggling, she slapped away his hand and made dramatic kissing sounds with her deep blue lips as she absentmindedly dropped one shiny shoe.

Their crude excitement cut Wally to the core. Reaching into his pocket with his right hand, he fingered the corkscrew. Clutching a chardonnay wine bottle in his left, he tightened his grip on the neck. When the two love drunks fell into the office, Wally fell in right behind them.

Closing the door, he said, "The prize-winning chardonnay you ordered has arrived, sir."

The woman cheered, pulled up the hem of her already short skirt and did a little dance. Delgado didn't remember ordering wine but wasn't about to turn down a gift or a wasted woman who wanted another drink and a raw good time. After all, this was wine country. And he was California's next governor. Whoever sent the scrawny wine delivery boy knew who was boss. Delgado liked that.

"My friends call me Sexy Chica," the woman said to Wally.

Wally's brain went numb.

"Ooooh, chica sexy," Syrah said.

"What the fuck?" said El Maloso from where he stood in the used car lot across the street.

Incredulous, one of his two gang soldiers slapped himself in the forehead.

"Who's the cue ball head who just barged into the office with those two pendejos?"

"Let's find out," El Maloso said.

Running across West Main Street and opening the unlocked door, the bad guy and his boys easily glided in, closing the door behind them.

"We're here to register to vote," El Maloso said.

"We want to volunteer on your campaign," said one of the soldiers.

"So we can apply for security jobs at the governor's mansion," said the other.

Delgado smelled his own fear.

El Maloso closed the cheap drapes Delgado had instructed staffers to hang on the picture window so he could use the office for campaign trail sexcapades

"Let's open that wine, gabacho," El Maloso said, using the term for a white person that can be said with love or distain.

Wally reached into his pocket.

"I just happen to have a corkscrew," he said.

The door opened.

Jesús Zarate stepped into the room.

"I know you," said Wally.

"Well, look who it is," said El Maloso. "El Coyote himself."

On his way to pick up vegetarian breakfast tacos at the all-night tortilleria, Jesús recognized Wally and his van from the field rally for Delgado and remembered seeing Father Fresa get in his VW bus that day. He was the same skinny little man he met sitting zazen on the beach. Jesús knew something was up when he spotted Delgado and friend, Wally and El Maloso and company all go in the same campaign door.

"I know you," said one of El Maloso's local enforcers, pointing at the woman with Delgado.

"My brother is Pepe," she said. "You were at my quinceañera."

Smart as he was—you don't get to be the Los Angeles-based president of Los Matadores by being the burro—El Maloso looked puzzled.

"Pepe is one of us here in Santa Maria," the cholo said.

Pointing to the woman, he said, "She sometimes hides our guns. We call her 'Super Chola. She probably already picked Delgado's pocket."

"This is easy," El Maloso said, pointing to the young woman.

"Put his wallet back. Then go home. You weren't here."

Pointing to Wally he said, "Open the wine."

Wally was getting the hang of the tool and a quick few turns of the wrist was all it took to uncork the bottle.

"Now, you two please leave us," El Maloso said to Wally and Jesús. "The campaign office doesn't open for a few hours. We loyal volunteers have a lot of work to do."

"Democracy never sleeps," Jesús said. "We weren't here, by the way."

"None of us were here," El Maloso said, placing his hand on Delgado's shoulder.

One by one, the chola gang girl—minus Delgado's fat wallet —Wally and Jesús left the room. Looking around headquarters, El Maloso found a stack of paper cups on a table decorated with red, white and blue crepe paper. Picking up three cups he filled them with wine.

"What about me?" Delgado asked. "I could use a drink, too."

El Maloso placed a cup in front of Delgado. Walking to the corner of the room, he picked up a case of "Fresa Te Amo" strawberry aftershave lotion that Delgado handed out to his donors. Pulling a bottle from the case, El Maloso opened the aftershave, filled a cup and pushed the drink in front of Delgado.

"To Carlos Delgado's poor choice of gangs to slander and blame for a homicide he committed, to a hot time in hell for burning a man of God and, mostly, to the fields."

El Maloso tilted his chardonnay, finished the drink in four consecutive swallows, and left.

Fifteen minutes later his cell phone rang.

"I am having terrible abdominal pain," Delgado said.

"Have another drink of the strawberry surprise," El Maloso said.

Ten minutes later his phone rang again.

"My eyes burn, my head aches, I am vomiting blood."

"A tu salud," El Maloso said, toasting Delgado's health.

Five minutes later another call came in.

"Your speech is slurred," El Maloso said. "You sound like you are in a stupor. You are dizzy and confused. But the bar is still open, Governor. Please drink up. Celebrate your electoral success."

The calls stopped when Delgado's heart stopped from ethyl and isopropyl alcohol poisoning induced by an overdose of potent strawberry aftershave

The last call came from Pepe.

"Where do you want us to dump him?" he asked. "The man can't hold his alcohol. But he sure smells nice."

"Time for a long walk off a short pier," El Maloso said.

"What do you want us to do with his ears?"

"Send them to his wife. With a note signed, 'Always, Los Matadores.' "

"Olé."

HELP ME, WALLY

"**W**ALLY, you want to tell me what were you doing at Delgado's campaign headquarters at 5 o'clock in the morning?" Jesús said. "With a bottle of snob wine, no less. You don't strike me as a chardonnay man."

Biting into his vegetarian taco, Wally dripped beans, rich white cheese, green salsa and habanero peppers drenched in lime juice and Tapatio. Nothing tasted as good since Lupe's birthday party.

"I'd rather not talk about it if you don't mind."

"That's not you, Wally. We just met really, but silence is definitely not you. You are a man looking for truth. A seeker. You must want to tell the truth."

"Okay."

"You came for revenge."

"No, justice."

"I can dig that. To punish?"

"No, to avenge."

"Words mean something to you, Wally. Respect does too."

"I try my best to make my mother proud."

"Getting even isn't always bad, Wally."

"You sound like you know what you're talking about."

"If you fight evil and protect what is good, your actions are part of the vital life force that is the universe. The Japanese call the power ki. The Chinese talk of chi. Yoga teachers call the energy prana. Warriors welcome attacks as gifts. We must know the difference between lusting for blood and fighting back because we must."

"I want to fight back," Wally said. "But sometimes I can't control myself."

"That's part of the way, learning discipline, taking responsibility."

"Syrah won't let me."

"Who?"

Wally shivered, put his face into his hands, and in seconds changed into someone else. Mesmerized, Jesús watched Wally's demeanor split in half. Facial features distorted. A smile turned to a sneer. Words hurled from his mouth instead of rolling gently from his lips. Amid this twisted rage, Jesús saw Wally for what dwelled deep inside an otherwise milquetoast—a real-life male devil.

"Back off taco breath," Syrah said. "You want those baby blues to twist at the end of a corkscrew?"

Jesús' knew. Who threatens your eyeballs? Could Wally be the Corkscrew Killer? Did this timid puppy have it in him to be the Central Coastal Corkscrewer?

"Nice to meet you, Syrah," Jesús said.

"I know your type," she said. "You got chardonnay drinker tight ass written all over you."

Wally made a small move toward his pants pocket. Jesús stood in a single swift movement, stepping away from the picnic table and turning his body sideways. In a volatile daze of inner turmoil, Wally hyperventilated. His mouth and face changed and he whimpered as he struggled to suck in air.

"Help me, Wally," Syrah said. "I'm afraid of all these fucking Mexicans."

Expecting a full-scale attack but trying to head off the charge, Jesús wanted to draw out Syrah more than she expected or wanted, playing on whatever weakness he might manipulate in Wally's short-circuited brain waves.

"Why the corkscrew?" he said. "Pretty grisly stuff."

"Wine enthusiasts can be extreme," Syrah said.

"Do you only kill in self-defense?"

"Chardonnay always warrants the death penalty."

"That explains wild Wayne Wilson, but what about the German deviate and the ditzy realtor?"

"Chard guzzlers as well," Syrah said. "They're all alike. Don't forget Poppy. Wayne was the worst, though—destroyed Wally's mother, turned his back on his son. Wally should have stuck and plucked him a long time before he did."

"Wayne was Wally's father."

"That porn couple hurt people too. Wally knew they weren't nice people. Wally always says it's nice to be nice and real men respect women."

"You agree with that, Syrah? It's nice to be nice? It's nice to be nice," Jesús said. "It's nice to be nice, Wally. It's nice to be nice."

Wally's eyes fluttered. Coming around like a punchy KO'd prizefighter struggling to one knee, Wally rubbed eyes glassy as antique cane-cut tournament marbles.

"I was dreaming," Wally said. "We were sitting on cushions in a monastery. My mother was chanting. Sandalwood incense burned. Shakuhachi music played. My mantra hummed in my head. It's nice to be nice. It's nice to be nice."

"You want to do something nice, Wally?"

"I do."

"You think you can handle early morning yoga class?"

THOUGHT HE SAW A COYOTE

Too tired and hungover to crawl from his sleeping bag, Animal pissed himself in the comfort of his own burrow, fouling his nest without a care or second thought. Members of the Crushers motorcycle club often pissed on each other's legs for fun as they stood at the bar. Once the stream started you weren't supposed to react, just stand there and take it like a man. Biker rules meant manners at the most inopportune times. With such training, extreme adaptation shaped the backbone of Animal's survival.

After lucking out and locating the two escapees after just a few days and leaving them a steaming message outside their motel room, a good night's sleep in a drainage ditch refreshed and recharged Animal. When the expression, "Does a bear shit in the woods?" crossed his mind for no good reason, Animal chuckled and reached into his saddle bag for a warm Coors. Shaking the can, he popped the top, spraying foam into his face and wiping a meaty paw across his eyes. With beer in his hair and piss in his pants, Animal crawled from his bag, stood with a groan and lumbered to his bike— one righteous biker on his way to another day at the beach.

If strategy went according to plan, the clash between him and Wallace and Rose would end by sundown. Warfare would cease. The Crushers would regain their status and rule Southern California without dissent. Animal saw himself as the new president of the club, wearing a new patch on faded colors that simply said, "Prez."

Usually unemotional to a fault, Animal couldn't wait to get even with that bitch Rose. When Wallace tried to intervene, he planned to cut off the traitor's testicles and make up a big pot of spaghetti and meatballs for Rose to have for supper before he tortured and gutted her like a white-tail deer—maybe give her a new kitten to take with her to her tomb. Yeah, a last meal of spaghetti and Wallace's balls sounded great. Maybe he'd have a plate with her, scarf down a pile of pasta and a fresh numb nut to show Rose how a real carnivore lets it all hang out when it comes to table manners and a romantic candlelit dinner.

The plan was simple: Follow the refugees at a watchful distance until he had an opening. Hunt them down like foaming-at-the-mouth mad dogs and capture them at gunpoint. Kill and cut Wallace, dissecting him like a biology laboratory specimen. Feed, fondle and finalize his last kiss with Rose before saying goodbye forever.

Then head back to Lompoc where he planned to expand the Crushers north to Oakland and the Bay Area and south to Tijuana. Fuck the Hells Angels and the Mongols. Crushers would rule. Maybe even move into Mexico and Oregon. Go all the way to the Canadian border. Challenge the Pagans and everybody else on the East Coast, too. Expand to Germany. Maybe Russia.

Fifteen minutes later, parked in the shadows of a shedding purple jacaranda tree, Animal heard the familiar roar of Wallace's motorcycle and watched the runaways flash by. Rose had her head buried deep into Wallace's shoulder and her arms wrapped tightly around his waist. Animal thought he was having an acid flashback because Rose and Wallace looked like they were wearing unisex dance tights like he saw the douchebags wearing on "Dance Party," the local TV show his old lady liked to watch when she was stoned.

Following at a discreet distance, Animal watched Wallace pull into a small strip mall in Shell Beach. Stepping off the bike, Animal saw he was wearing sweatpants and a tank top. Sonofabitch if Rose wasn't wearing rainbow-colored tights of some kind. Animal liked her better in a white waitress uniform. Painted in colorful pastels across the studio entrance, "Yoga Zero" caught Animal's eye. Thinking they must be going in to stick up the joint, Animal pulled away and found a place where he could park, watch and track them when they left.

By the time Animal opened a beer and snorted two lines of homemade methamphetamine, a 1963 Lincoln low-rider followed by a 1966 VW van pulled into adjacent parking spaces on the street. Animal watched a gawky string bean with a shaved head, bell-bottom jeans and a tie-dyed T-shirt get out of the van's driver's side. A long-haired older man about 45 with broad shoulders and an edge to his gait jumped from the driver's side of his low-rider. Together they breezed into the yoga studio, looking confident, like they were walking on air.

Out of the corner of his eye, Animal thought he saw a mighty coyote rip across the 101 freeway and disappear over the guard rail. Listening to the wind, Animal heard a devil scream. Sky colors turned black and blue. Life cut to a dream.

TOPLESS PUBLISHER

KCOY 12 set up a television satellite truck outside Sinaloa Lucy's famous nail shop to interview the star witness before she got her manicure.

"We're live in Santa Maria with an eyewitness who says she saw Republican gubernatorial candidate Carlos Delgado drive past her at 10 a.m. this morning in his yellow Silverado. What exactly did you see, Miss?"

The flirtatious gang accomplice feigned surprise.

"I wasn't expecting the press," she said with a wiggle and a giggle.

Sexy Chica snapped her chewing gum.

"Governor Delgado was blowing kisses at me, right? That's how I know it was him. He does that all the time when he sees me, right? That Santa Maria Mirror newspaper publisher girl was sitting beside him in the truck as they rolled by. She was like topless, right? Let it all hang out topless, right? Wearing a straw cowboy hat and waving a bottle of chardonnay out the passenger side window. I know it was chard because the color of the wine matched the color of her ponytail except for the roots. The words "Vegas or Bust" were written in red lipstick in big letters across her tits. I never been to Vegas. But I couldn't miss the bust part. Get it? Ha. That's a joke, mami."

"You're sure it was them?"

"I know him, everybody knows him, and I saw her with him once before at the Bronc Buster Motel screw pit out on Blosser Road, checking in drunk and checking out an hour later more drunk. I was working as a housekeeper making beds and shit."

"Please, Miss, you cannot say shit on live television news."

"Sorry. They were drunk and holding each other up after a quickie."

"Serving beer in Tijuana was more dignified than this shit," the reporter said. "Back to you, Ricardo."

Dropping the mic, the reporter walked off-camera.

Pepe laughed so hard he choked watching his sister on TV—a natural at helping cover Los Matadores' tracks in the disappearance of Delgado. So what if he and his homies had to grab that snotty newspaper publisher and dump her to make the story work. Nobody would miss her, anyway. They simply drove over to her house in Delgado's yellow pickup with him stiff, earless and wrapped in a tarp in the truck bed, knocked on her door and told her the candidate needed to talk with her immediately. In a matter of seconds she was squealing in the extra deep and wide cross-body toolbox that was big enough to hold half-a-steer to barbecue and cut into Santa Maria-style instant heart attack Chamber of Commerce-style tri-tip sandwiches.

At 3:14 a.m. with no eyewitnesses, Pepe, a demolition derby champion at the Santa Maria Speedway and aspiring Hollywood stunt man, hit 85 miles per hour before diving out of the truck cab and into the ocean as the shiny Silverado went off the edge of the deserted Harford Pier in Avila Beach and slammed into deep still water. Within 10 minutes the truck hit bottom in deep murky water. One hour later Pepe and his boys were at the clubhouse chugging Sol beers and grilling fresh oysters with salt, Tapatio and limón.

Back in his cool East LA casa, El Maloso slipped on a purple and black silk robe and drank an ice cold horchata rice drink with cinnamon to which he added a shot of mescal. After cleaning his guns he prepared for bed. Going to sleep happy made El Maloso ready for tomorrow. No telling who might need killing. Los Matadores always took credit for the shit they did. Nobody blamed them for shit they didn't do and lived, let alone get elected governor.

Pase buenas noches.

Good night.

And don't forget to vote.

EL MAL DE OJO

A LL people feel the power of yesterday.

On that day decades ago, cries came in the morning. Cries came in the evening. Since the day she was born all the baby seemed to do was cry—more than she ate or performed any other infantile function. Beautiful in white lace outfits, 6-month-old Zita's tears for the past week represented a dark force in the child's abundant spirit that spurred her mother to action.

"A spell," said Juana Lopez. "Someone who knows of her birth has looked at my niña with an evil eye."

Neighbors on her dirt street in Benito Juarez, Oaxaca, stood by helplessly, breathing rapidly, afraid of what might come next— good, decent people who knew Juana, respected her compassion for them, and wanted to help but did not know what to do. A good neighbor in this mountain village, Juana Lopez always helped those in need. So it came as no surprise when people rejoiced when she gave birth to a baby girl with tiny midnight stars twinkling in her stunning onyx eyes.

"Do not worry," Juana said. "I will heal her tears."

Producing a smooth, unbroken brown egg from the fold of her apron, she rubbed the shell over the child's downy black hair. Moving the egg over the baby's face and neck, she covered the entire length of the baby's body. Each precious tiny toe received the same meticulous attention. And when she was through, she broke the egg into a tall clear glass. People gasped at the tiny chicken embryo that plopped into the glass and now floated yolky yellow amid thick albumen. The sprouting pecker head showed the start of a beak and squinty bitty eyes that looked awake and piercing.

"Garcia," a woman whispered before she fainted.

"The chicken looks like Garcia," a man hissed. "Garcia made this child suffer."

No one disagreed that the chicken fetus looked like the drunken man who beat his wife and children in the cinder block house across the street. No one disputed the wickedness that lived in Garcia's black heart.

When Juana Lopez kissed her child on her left cheek the baby stopped crying.

When Juana kissed Zita on her right cheek the baby smiled.

One hour later as Juana breastfed Zita, Garcia's wife screamed when she stumbled across her husband lying facedown in the slop where the loafing pigs lived behind the house that now belonged to her.

So many years later, Zita told the story in America as if she witnessed the events herself—which she did although she was much too young to recall detail. In her telling of the tale she swore she saw it all from above, as if she were looking down on the scene that provided the first vision of her calling.

"Did my abuela kill Garcia?" then-25-year-old Jesús asked his mother.

"No," Zita said. "Garcia killed himself with his own mal de ojo. His own evil eye looked back at him."

"Did abuela help him die?"

"Yes, she was always willing to help those in need."

"Do you help people die?"

"Please, mijo."

"Do you help them die?"

"If they need my help to die, I help them die. But I will help you live," Zita said. "Just as Jesús Malverde will help you live. We will both help you live."

With that kind of backing, eventually no one could stop this young fighter for the people. But Jesús did not yet know he was a direct descendant of the famous champion. Until he did, he was on his own, cutting his own path through an uncompromising life.

A woman of her word, Zita Lopez helped everyone who needed her power until the day she disappeared. Now Jesús could only see and hear his mother in his dreams. The night she first came to him as a face in his prison cell, he realized the dreams were now their only way to communicate. Jesús knew she was out there somewhere, alive, on her own. He just didn't know where or why she left him. The emptiness gave Jesús time to ponder his lonely existence.

From the time he was small, friends of his mother called him "the messenger." Las brujas, the witches he came to know in the barrio, called him "El Coyote," just like the lean carnivores that moved closer and closer each day into the heart of the city. Tricky survivors, coyotes displayed attributes that helped them stay alive. The witches knew Jesús would need those skills as well. The witches knew he was destined to be a beautiful beast.

Growing up Jesús played soccer and boxed with his friends in the backyard. He laughed loudly and ate tacos and french fries like most children his age. He read books from the children's library and finger painted in school. He liked low-rider cars, nice girls and yappy Chihuahuas—dragonflies, too. Scorpions and birds were his favorites. Jesús loved all animals.

He also took great pride in being Mexican, not Mexican-American but Mexican, even though his mother gave birth in the USA, taking comfort in his heritage even though he only knew half his bloodline.

The mystical side was more elusive.

Smart and introspective as a teenager, Jesús noticed growing powers of speed and smell. At dinner he tore through the blood and gristle of a rare steak. He nurtured strong genes, his roots and life itself. At no time did Jesús believe he possessed special gifts or a human resolve capable of ancient magic. At night when he dreamed, often running on all fours in those visions, snarling and growling and sometimes worse, Jesús always awoke refreshed, strong and ready to run again. Lucid sleep images provided a brilliant never-ending cycle that energized him, forging a savage desire to survive.

Jesús found innocent strength in nature, not in the occult. But on those nightly runs he felt ferocious, haunted by the earthy smell of the hunt and an uncivilized confidence when coyote mind enveloped him and took over—roaming wild, free and dangerous, fatal to any enemy that crossed his path.

Jesús rode celestial dreams that would teach a sharp truth about his fierce agility and breeding that flowed through his veins as he endured and passed through time. Like any primal howl from a fur-covered mammal, his voice drew from a primitive past. Destiny's phantom, he answered an otherworldly call, a plea to save the world from evil.

Ghosts of the dead called his name.

Jesús Zarate answered.

DOWNWARD-FACING WALLY

CANDLELIGHT flickered from four corners of the room. Breathing slowed. A single thin stick of green pine-scented Japanese incense stuck into a pottery bowl filled with sand burned red at the tip, creating serenity in the minds and bodies of the yoginis who stretched out on thin multi-colored rubber mats rolled out in the yoga studio.

"The corpse pose is alive," said Tibetty, the yoga instructor.

Thin as a sitar string, Tibetty wore a blue and yellow glass bead necklace that hung to her waist and bounced against her tanned belly button. Rings on her fingers and bells on her toes shimmered in the shadows.

"The corpse pose is alive and well in your personal solar system that lives forever," she said. "Salute your sun."

Wally saluted, snapping his fingers to his temple like a Marine Corps honor guard.

"Slut," Syrah whispered. "You want a corpse pose? We'll give you a corpse pose."

"Shhhhh," hissed Wally. "Please, Syrah."

Tibetty seemed intrigued by the hissing—like a cobra had secretly wriggled into class—but hadn't understood the words Wally suddenly spit in a husky, high-pitched female voice. Calmly re-establishing her focus, Tibetty adjusted deeper into full lotus position and leaned forward. In one smooth motion she flipped waist-length purple and black hair over her shoulder. Beatific, she beamed, tickled with her ability to commune with the cosmos.

Jesús stretched out with his legs extended and arms palm-up

by his side.

"Inhale slowly, mindfully," Tibetty said. "Inhale and feel the oxygen flow from your center, your hara, as the vital life force slips into your brain. Exhale. When life molecules arrive in your brain, ask them to dance. They do the swim. They do the twist. They mashed potato, too. Breathe. Become a single atom. This is the key to the universe. Open your doors of perception."

In the ballroom of his mind Wally twisted. Jesús performed a Mexican stomp he learned as a boy from his neighbors. Wallace swam and Rose hully-gullied. Syrah did the mashed potatoes.

"Namaste," Tibetty said.

"Namaste," said most of the class.

In the parking lot Jesús shook hands with Rose and Wallace.

"Nice to see you again," he said. "Yoga class is always better than kicking ass."

"Peace, love and vegetables, right?" Rose said.

Turning to Wally, Jesús threw a thumb his way and said, "My new amigo, Wally."

"Dude, you're, like, glowing," Rose said.

Embarrassed, Wally looked at his hands and outstretched fingers.

"I'm on fire," he said.

"I feel like a fish taco," Jesús said. "You two want to get something to eat with me and Wally?"

A low-rider cruiser followed by a vintage VW bus followed by a custom Harley-Davidson is nothing new on the windy road to Avila Beach. Neither is a second Harley following closely, but not too closely, as the twists and turns lead to Pete's pierside seafood shack, complete with pigeons, plastic chairs, barking sea lions and a green, blue and gold coastal view unmatched anywhere in California.

"What are you drinking?" Jesús asked.

Rose looked at Wallace. Wallace looked at Rose.

"Water for us," she said.

Jesús came back with water and made-from-scratch wine coolers for himself and Wally.

"When I was little, my mother made homemade wine from

Spanish plums and drank it with fresh limes, lemons and a shot of cactus juice," Jesús said.

"What did your dad drink?" Wally said.

"I never knew him," Jesús said.

"Me, neither," Wallace said. "I mean I didn't know my dad either."

"Your mothers raised you?" Rose asked.

Jesús and Wallace nodded.

"Mine, too," Wally said.

All eyes turned to Wally.

"Mommy was a hippie," he said. "An earth mother like Janis Joplin, but I wasn't Jim Morrison's love child. She got sick and drank aftershave lotion once. Always loved me and took care of me. Said I could go to the prom my senior year with my girlfriend Miriam."

Wally took a long pull on his fruity wine cooler.

"My mother's name was Miriam," Wallace said.

"It's a pretty name," Rose said. "Did you have a good time at the prom, Wally?"

"We couldn't go," Wally said. "Something happened to Miriam. We couldn't go."

"I'm sorry, Wally," Rose said.

"No, it's okay," Wally said. "I never saw Miriam again. She disappeared. Her father told me not to call or he'd murder me."

Gull squawks and sea lion barks filled the empty space in Wally's desolation.

"Other than memories, all I have to remember Miriam is this," Wally said.

Pulling a worn, cracked leather wallet from the back pocket of his jeans, he dug deep. Encased in yellowed plastic, Miriam's senior picture appeared in remarkably good shape for the years he carried it everywhere he went.

"This is my Miriam," Wally said.

Rose carefully slid the photo from Wally's fingers.

"Miriam is beautiful," she said, handing the photo to Jesús.

"Looks gentle and mellow," he said, passing the picture to Wallace.

For one uncomfortably long minute Wallace did nothing but stare. Politely handing the photograph back to Wally, he pushed back his plastic chair, stood and pulled up the collar of his faded blue denim jacket.

"Later," he said.

By the time Rose caught up, Wallace had already kicked over the bike's engine and was revving the motor like a fleeing felon. Rose wasn't sure if he was laughing or crying. But she was smart enough not to ask.

"I need a drink," Wallace said.

Distracted and dismayed, they tore away from the pier parking lot. Animal pulled out behind them.

"Namaste, my ass," he said.

WORSE THAN HIS BITE

SPITTING on his detective's badge, Gagliardi used his snotty handkerchief to polish the gold shield to a bright sheen. Hooking the badge on his belt, he checked his Glock and secured the gun into his shoulder holster. Gagliardi's belly growled.

"I'm so hungry I could eat an illegal alien," he said out loud to himself.

A prisoner once wisecracked on hearing Gagliardi's hungry stomach growl and paid dearly.

"Time to skin the cat, detective," the prisoner said. "You Swiss Italians are cat eaters, I hear."

Gagliardi turned in the squad car driver's seat and shot the prisoner three times in the chest. Then he drove the body to the fields and dumped it behind a broccoli floret harvester truck. When he responded the next morning to a report of a "broccoli field killing," he wrote in his official police report that death resulted from "a wetback drug assassination because broccolis can't shoot."

The cops at the station laughed for days. But nobody suggested Gagliardi change the report. Nobody fucked with a cat eater.

This morning Mrs. Delgado came to the police station and turned over the package she received in the mail. Tough as Gagliardi thought he was, he gagged when he opened the box that once contained a set of crystal tequila glasses suitable for a wedding gift. Two severed ears resembling stale chicharrones, pork rinds complete with brown bristly hairs sticking out of the dead skin pores, rested on a bloody patch of cotton.

"You gonna take prints off them?" Mrs. Delgado asked.

"Yeah, sure, I'm going to dust them personally, hold each one up to the light to make sure I don't miss a loop or a whirl. Are you fucking nuts? I'll send them to the lab and they'll throw them in the garbage. What do you think we are, Forensic Files on TV?"

"How about the FBI? They'll investigate because he was an elected official. Terrorism, maybe. The Russian government. The Russian Mafia.

"MS-13, 14 and 15 gang initiation. Simple as that, case closed."

"Don't you want to know who did this?"

"No."

"Yeah, me neither."

"Your husband was an asshole. The more I think about it, the more I know we're both better off without him. With pictures of his ears as evidence of his demise, you get a nice insurance settlement whether his body is found or not. I get freedom to do as I please, pick up some of the loose ends he left hanging around."

What Gagliardi didn't tell Mrs. Delgado was that he also had a key to her husband's safety deposit box loaded with a million in cash he used to spend on his harem of girlfriends. By tomorrow Gagliardi would be headed to Reno to see the Rod Stewart concert and start a harem of his own.

What Mrs. Delgado didn't tell Gagliardi was that she already cashed out the safety deposit box with a key of her own. Also, she had the secret surveillance video of the detective beating and stabbing the priest to death that her husband secured and left on his home computer she checked for his girlfriends' messages every time that dirty, cheating bastard left the house. She already emailed a copy of the video to Jesús Zarate, the crusading, long-haired and now unemployed newspaper columnist her husband hated.

Gagliardi started to sing some Rod Stewart about wanting his body.

"Speaking of bodies, do you know where the rest of my husband's body is?"

"Maybe ground up in the taco truck specials for the next week."

"That's good," Mrs. Delgado said.

"That's good? Why is that?" Gagliardi said.

"They can serve my poor husband's meat to you crooked Swiss Italian cops when you run out of pussy cat for lunch."

THE BIGGEST COYOTE ROSE EVER SAW

DEEP in the coyote's chest, a growl grew like the opening notes of a husky song of survival. Intensifying, the sound swelled with a sense of dominance. Building like rolling thunder before turning to killer lightening, anarchy grew to unleash death in the coiled spring of the predator's hunt. The coyote moved quickly, unseen and parallel to Animal, stalking him as prey as he stalked his targets.

"Okay, fuckers," Animal said. "Payback is a bitch."

With an open Buck Knife in each hand, Animal waited all day, lurking outside the Sea Urchin before spotting Wallace and Rose exit the motel after dark and walk down the street. Following them six blocks at a distance, Animal watched them enter Shell Beach Wine Beer & Spirits. Parking in the back and creeping to the open door, he listened to the din and crackle of her words as Rose tried and failed to talk Wallace out of his purchase.

"You promised," she said. "You promised."

The couple had argued nonstop after leaving the pier. Despite a long nap to escape his depression and help give him time to make a decision, Wallace decided to get drunk anyway. Rose decided to give up. They watched the 10 o'clock news in tense silence and left the room together the same miserable way.

After paying for his purchase, Wallace carried a bottle of Rebel Yell bourbon in each hand, stomping with purpose out to Shell Beach Road when a fast-moving blur made him duck and lose his balance.

Animal bear-hugged Wallace's back with an animal on his back. A primeval howl bit into the soft night air. Blood flew everywhere, spattering Wallace's face as he saw a glint of steel flash from two broad knives. More blood pumped from Animal's open gashes produced by what in the frenzy looked like paws, claws and fangs dripping red and white foamy saliva.

Rose screamed.

Wallace fell to the street, trying to rise in a frantic motion when the flesh of Animal's neck opened wide, exposing the cervical spinal cord that connected to muscles, nerves and vertebrae. Carotid arteries gushed. Silver trachea cartilage and red muscle glistened wet in the glow of the red and orange neon liquor sign.

Desperately trying to throw Animal's body off his back, Wallace gave a mighty heave at the same time Rose pulled Animal by the hair from behind. Because of his soon-to-be-mortal wounds, most of Animal's scalp came off in Rose's hand. With gray matter exposed and Animal's heart pulsing its final few beats, Rose watched his brain quiver, shut down and die.

The monster that killed him disappeared as quickly as it pounced.

"Oh, my god," Rose said. "That was the biggest coyote I ever saw."

Breathing in short spurts, Wallace could barely speak.

"No," he said. "No. Animal was swinging two razor-sharp knives. He must have accidently cut himself. Me, or somebody else, somehow turned those blades around on him. I didn't see any coyote."

Rose's panic level rose as did her volume.

"Yes, you did, Wallace. You saw a humongous fucking coyote, Wallace, same as me."

How could a gargantuan coyote pounce in Shell Beach at midnight and kill in such a swift gory fashion? Maybe the attacker just looked like a coyote, a guardian angel that saved his life. Wallace wanted to run but had nowhere to go. Wallace didn't know what to think.

"Look at him," Rose said. "Ripped apart like Meat-Eaters Week on the National Geographic Channel."

Two Buck Knives lay on either side of the body. Shredded cords in Animal's neck left a thick pool of blood on the macadam. Animal lost the top of his head in the attack. What was left of his scalp resembled a road kill skunk.

A siren blew in the distance. Rose opened the saddle bags on Animal's motorcycle and grabbed a leather-fringed pouch she spotted resting at the top. Knowing a personal drug bag when she saw one, she hid the stash under her arm. In the adrenaline-rushed aftermath of the death dance, Wallace failed to notice.

Rose and Wallace sat on the edge of the bed in their motel room when the first squad car arrived on the scene. Wallace got a glass from the bathroom and poured four fingers of Rebel Yell. Rose opened the tan fringe bag loaded with crystal meth and poured out four lines.

"You want some of this?" she said pointing to the dope.

"You want some of this?" he said pointing to the bourbon.

Rose took the glass.

Wallace leaned over the dresser and snorted two lines of crank.

"Like I don't have enough on my mind, but what am I going to do about Miriam?" Wallace said.

"You mean Wally's girlfriend?"

"Yeah," Wallace said. "I mean Wally's girlfriend, who happens to be my mother."

THE SPITTING IMAGE

"So how do you explain mister badass biker's rudeness?" asked Syrah.

"Maybe he was just having a bad day," Wally said.

Wally boiled tofu hot dogs in a pot on a Coleman gas cook stove he set up in the VW camper. Slices of white bread and yellow mustard made Wally feel like a pioneer, a rugged individual on an adventure that petrified and exhilarated him at the same time.

"All you did was show Miriam's picture and he went pale as seagull shit and stormed off the pier. You even picked up the tab," Syrah said.

"Rose apologized for him," Wally said.

"Rose was embarrassed and didn't know what happened either."

"Wallace is an outlaw biker. Outlaw bikers act irrationally at times."

"He looked like he wanted to kill you. Maybe it's time you punch his ticket, Wally. I wonder if he's a chardonnay drinker."

'Syrah, please. Take a deep breath, okay?"

"You know who he looks like, Wally?" Syrah asked.

Now Wally went pale. He immediately noticed the resemblance but did everything in his power to ignore the striking similarity. Strange shit happened in California all the time. Wally sometimes looked at himself in the mirror and thought he looked like Wavy Gravy from Woodstock, so it shouldn't surprise anybody if somebody else looked like him.

"Wallace is the spitting image of you," Syrah said. "Got those same basket case eyes."

"Stop, Syrah."

"Same fleshy neck and pasty complexion."

"Stop."

"And what's with the second coming of our lord and savior? What about this Jesús?"

"Jesús is my friend," Wally said. "He's trying to help me. I appreciate his effort. He said I can get better if I want to, if I really try. He said...."

"He said I'm the problem and if I disappear you'll feel better, right? Is that what the beaner bastard said about me, Wally?"

"He didn't say it like that, Syrah. And don't be racist."

"We're in this together, Wally. Where you go I go. We're everything together. Separate we're nothing. You can't live without me, Wally. Remember that."

Wally remembered.

"You saw where rugged old-fashioned American individuality got that priest friend of yours."

Reaching for his corkscrew, Wally heard bongos.

THE COYOTE

Like the last morning after he killed, Jesús awoke with blood on his hands—all the way up his arms to his elbows. This time, though, drying, sticky blood caked everywhere else as well. Blood covered his shirt and pants. Blood masked his face, coated his neck and clotted in his hair. Blood stained his teeth.

What he remembered from the night before was spotting the Crusher pull out on his bike behind Wallace and Rose when he ran after them at the pier. Yelling goodbye to Wally and that he would meet up with him later, Jesús jumped in the Lincoln and tailed the barbarian biker who was tailing Wallace and Rose. Then he watched him all day until the maniac made his move later that night.

Trying to retrace his steps, Jesús closed his eyes. Falling into a black and white dream that now regularly overtook reality, he drifted deeper and deeper into the jungle of his soul, greeting his mother, father and grandmother as they stepped into view to guide him on his path.

In this fantasy the smell is overpowering—a fetid, human scent, rank and warm. Vulnerable, his prey is oblivious to the presence of the hunter. Careless, big, dumb and easy game, his quarry makes the kill too easy. The coyote throws back his head and opens wide jaws that expose sharp pointed spikes.

When the man called Animal moves in for the kill, the coyote moves in for his. Animal loses two knives he grips as soon as the first paw catches him behind the ear, opening up the trapezius and lacerating the scalp. The second swipe is the equivalent of three big bites of the Adam's apple, continuing through his chin and tearing both lips from his face. Hungry now, the coyote sinks his teeth into his victim's shoulder, biting and wrestling thick deltoid muscle, violently shaking his head, ripping flesh for a midnight snack before moving on into the night.

Snapping back to consciousness, Jesús sat up quickly. Sweating profusely, he slid out of bed in one smooth motion and walked slowly to the bathroom. Stepping into the shower, he turned on the hot water and stood beneath its spray until he could no longer take the heat.

After his shower he stood in a towel, staring into the full refrigerator. Jesús had no appetite. So he popped a Pacifico beer and sat alone at the kitchen table, thinking through the godlike animal nature of his being that felt more dominant than ever.

El Coyote had come home.

Societal self-defense mattered. Jesús never started a fight but finished many. In his world no separation existed between man and beast, and now the beast seemed to have his back better than anyone.

"Here Regalo," he said, looking down at the red and black linoleum squares on the kitchen floor.

The Mexican bark scorpion responded to its name. Looking up, the scorpion curled its greenish yellow tail over its back and slowly moved toward its owner. Dangling slowly, deliberately, from the left and then to the right, the tail hung in the air ready to strike. Living up to its Spanish name—a present, a gift—Jesús' scorpion companion reminded Jesús of himself—a feared creature, sometimes mocked and always threatening.

Jesús kneeled, reached under the table and pulled out a cramped metal cage. Opening the small door, he inserted his hand and quickly snatched up a tiny white mouse by the tail.

"We are not mice, Regalo," he said to his pet as he dropped the struggling rodent onto the floor. "We will never be mice."

Turning his back, Jesús left the room, feeling bad for the mouse. Nobody escapes. We all eventually get eaten. Regalo cornered and captured his meal, feasting until his craving was complete. Then he scampered to a dark corner where he hid until he hungered for another ambush—another hunt for his own tough self-preservation, another lurking deception, a trap from which his prize could not escape.

Jesús did the same.

MOTHER

"You're sure it's her," Rose said.

"It's her high school yearbook picture."

"How do you know?"

"The photograph is all she kept from her past. I found it when she died," Wallace said. "The same one Wally carries."

"Where is your picture of her?"

"In my apartment."

"Firebombed and well done courtesy of the Crushers—if the TV news is accurate."

"Ashes to ashes, baby."

"Some high schools put old yearbooks online," Rose said.

"There's a computer for guests downstairs in the motel lobby," Wallace said.

The internet search ended quickly. Miriam posed for her senior photo with that Mona Lisa look she carried all her life and listed Drama Club as her only extracurricular activity. She listed her favorite saying as "I'm sorry." Wally's senior photo appeared on the very next page and listed no activities or favorite saying. Looking afraid, like somebody might hit him, Wally looked just like Wallace.

"Wally hasn't changed," Rose said.

"My mother changed by the second."

"Wally's nice but more than a little weird."

"Exactly my mother's type."

"Sort of like you."

"What's that supposed to mean?"

"Wally's got more than a little of you in him and you got more than a little of him in you."

"That's as gnarly as it gets."

"What happened outside the liquor store isn't?"

"Why didn't my mom tell me?"

"Miriam had her reasons."

"Why didn't Wally try to find me?"

"Maybe he didn't know."

Wallace took a few moments to think that one over.

"He'll know the next time I see him."

"Like we pencil him in our social calendar? Wallace, it's time to get out. Move on. A coyote on steroids ate a Crusher named Animal and we were there."

"I'm telling you for the last time. I didn't see super coyote."

"Then what slaughtered Animal?"

"Not what, Rose, who?"

"Okay, so who?"

"Jesús Zarate, that's who."

REST IN PEACE, PADRE

HOLDING aloft great gold candlesticks from their respective churches, a dozen Mexican-American altar boys and girls marched at the head of Father Fresa's funeral procession. Beginning on Broadway and heading down West Main Street, the procession ended at the strawberry field where the farmworkers agreed their priest would be buried—the field where Fresa confronted Delgado and bravely stood his ground.

The farmer who owned the land had agreed to fence off a plot where no berries would ever again be planted. The farmworkers planned to build a memorial bench suitable for meditation, personal reflection and prayer. Of course the donated land would be tax deductible and played for all it was worth for agribusiness public relations purposes. Still, the farmer empathized with the farmworkers. Had he not agreed to the simple proposal, El Matadores would have followed through on their friendly offer to burn down his business and his house. The farmer politely declined their offer and offered to help.

Holding the priest's simple wooden coffin aloft on their shoulders, six men including Wally—who Lupe's father invited to serve as a pall bearer—carried him down the center of the street. Other men carried satin banners and red and green flags bearing the likenesses of Christ, Jesús Malverde, the Virgin of Guadalupe, Santa Muerte and Father Fresa. A legion of women dropped flowers picked fresh from the fields on the street so the procession moved forward on a carpet of petals. Led by Lupe and dressed in their best clothes, an army of grieving children followed. Musicians walked in step, playing trumpets, tubas and drums. The paper reported more than 10,000 mourners.

"What a fucking circus," Gagliardi said to one of his lieutenants as they watched the coffin move forward.

"The reward for the priest's killer still on?" the underling said.

"No. Case closed," Gagliardi said.

Wally struggled to balance his friend's dead weight. Plodding along, he knew the others would cover for him if he failed, but Wally took pride in being asked and being able pull his share, to do his part in the symbolic and continuing struggle. Liberty and justice for all meant more to these undocumented Mexicans than it did to most native-born Americans.

Fairness appealed to Wally.

Nearing the open grave, Wally heard bongos—not timpanis, trombones, maracas or cowbells. Wally heard bongos.

Turning to the beat, he saw Gagliardi smirk and knew in his heart—as if a spiritual guide had pointed the way—that the priest's killer was laughing all the way to Father Fresa's grave. If Delgado's guilt covered him like slime—and it did—this butcher's scum reeked of a greater transgression. Now he would pay.

"Don't bless him, Father, for he has sinned," Wally said. "This is his first and last confession."

"What did you say, bitch?" Gagliardi said.

Jesús Zarate appeared out of nowhere.

"He said sin creates confusion, officer."

Gagliardi stepped back.

"I give the order and you're dead," he said. "I have snipers."

"And I have vipers—serpents that journeyed all the way from the flaming pits of Hell."

Jesús couldn't believe what just came out of his own mouth.

Wally gave him a strange look.

Gagliardi did not feel the thick snake that slowly slithered across the toe of the detective's black polished hand-tooled cowboy boot and curled snugly around his ankle.

Reaching into his pocket, Wally touched the sharp tip of his corkscrew.

Looking at Gagliardi, Wally hissed.

"Welcome to the Garden of Eden," Syrah said.

NICE TO BE NICE

Back at Pete's, a juvenile humpback whale had taken to lounging in the shallow water at the side of the pier that extends into San Luis Bay and leads to the ocean. Tourists from Fresno squealed and stumbled, clamoring for selfies and videos, almost pushing a San Luis television news crew over the edge. Sea lions barked. Gulls hovered. And four unlikely associates drawn together by fate and other quirky forces of nature faced off with an extreme mix of emotion.

"Time to talk," Jesús said.

"I saw you kill Animal," Wallace said.

"I saw a coyote kill Animal," Rose said.

"You're both right in seeing what you saw," Jesús said. "The mind sometimes acts of its own accord. Reality can mimic hypnotism."

"Did you kill Animal?" Rose asked.

"Yes, in defending you two."

"I saw a fucking coyote and that's that," Rose said.

"Father Fresa says a sin is not a sin if it erases a greater sin," Wally said.

All eyes flashed his way.

"You talk too fucking much," Syrah said.

"Holy shit," Rose said as she watched Wally's physical demeanor change and his voice take on the snide tone of sarcasm.

"What the fuck," Wallace said.

"Let her—and him—talk," Jesús said.

"It's nice to be nice and they weren't nice people," Wally said.

"Who, Wally?" Rose said. "Who wasn't nice?"

"The people Wally corkscrewed," Syrah said. "Thanks for the verb, Pancho Villa. Chardonnay drinkers all—the most pampered abuse of birthright on the coast."

"You admit you're the Corkscrew Killer and proud of it?" Jesús said.

Wally grinned.

"I'm sick," he said. "But the moral of the story is it's nice to be nice."

"Were you nice to Miriam?" Wallace asked.

Wally blushed.

"I loved her so much," he said. "I still do."

"Miriam's dead," Wallace said.

"Don't push your luck," Syrah said.

"Miriam was my mother," Wallace said.

Wally gasped and put his hand to his mouth.

"She told me how her father made her move to another town when she got pregnant with me," Wallace said. "How she missed her prom and graduation. My mother suffered so much to raise me and got sicker and sickest when I was a teenager. She wouldn't tell me who my father was because she said it was best he and I not know. Then she shot herself and killed what was left of my family."

"Miriam was going to have a baby?" Wally said. "Our baby?"

"You really didn't know?" Rose said.

Wally looked like he might pass out.

Wallace mirrored the image of his father.

"Dad?" he said. "Dad?"

Wally fainted.

STINSON BEACH

ALL now on the run together, about 69 miles into the trip north to Stinson Beach, the caravan pulled into the motel/restaurant/convenience store/gas station at Ragged Point.

"Pit stop," Jesús said.

Wallace and Rose parked behind him. Wally followed in the van. Syrah sulked, giving Wally the silent treatment.

"Gas up," Jesús said. "It's a beautiful day for a trip through Big Sur."

Wally reached into the handmade, rainbow-colored hippie bag he bought from a hitchhiker in Cambria, opened the case and slipped a disc into the customized CD slot. A psychedelic flute accompanied by bass and rocking psychedelic lyrics blasted to life through the bus's rebuilt and perfect sound system.

"You are something else, Wally," Rose said.

"My mother's music," he said.

Ragged Point marked the beginning of Big Sur, a rugged path up the coast unrivaled anywhere for natural splendor. With 279.7 miles to go to Stinson Beach, the road gypsies comprised a ragged bunch on their way to new lives and hopefully better times. Nobody in the small group disagreed that men and women wanted by a notorious outlaw motorcycle gang and trigger-happy cops had much of a chance unless they went underground fast.

"My mother loved Stinson Beach," Wally said. "She said the Dead and the Airplane lived there and they spread Janis Joplin's ashes on the beach after her memorial service."

Pulling a plastic bag half-full of sand from his black canvas knapsack that rested on the front seat, Wally poured a small amount of sand into a small green ceramic bowl he pulled from the knapsack as well. Sitting the bowl on the driver's seat, he poured sand to the top. Lighting a stick of Japanese incense he also pulled from his bag, nipping the flame with his thumb and forefinger, and touching the tip of the stick to his forehead the way he saw mountain monks do in a video, Wally spoke his personal words to live.

"Peace of mind," he said.

Sticking the unlit incense tip into the sand, he watched smoke curl into the fresh clean air and California sunshine.

"The sand is from Stinson Beach," he said. "Call it another little piece of Janis' heart."

"You are so lovable," Rose said before heading for the ladies' room.

In the men's room Wallace took two long pulls on a pint of Jack Daniel's. Next door Rose snorted lines of meth from toilet paper she put down on the top of the toilet bowl tank.

Leaning on the pump, Jesús gassed up the low-rider Lincoln and ate an ice cream sandwich. Time to hide out, regroup and plan his next move sounded good—as long as he could keep all these crazy fuckers in line, especially Syrah.

Good luck with that, he thought.

Good luck keeping himself together, too.

LOVE YOUR MOTHER

ABANDONED in the late '50s as a Boy Scout camp, the isolated location nestled in lower Northern California between Caspar and Russian Gulch State Park worked perfectly for an active service unit in a budding guerilla army. Tripper, a self-proclaimed tree hugger, ran the show with military precision, making a refuge for a nine-member female squad of far left, militant women who loved other species more than they loved humans because people create and carry out more danger to the planet.

The feds called their actions of the past three years eco-terrorism.

The Mother Earth Patrol (MEP) called their mission eco-patriotism.

Patriotism meant resisting through any means necessary the private property rights that damaged the natural world. Living the legacy of Amazons, warriors who banded together in kindred sisterhood and bonded in acts of strategic sabotage, these women defied capitalism and declared war on those who hurt Mother Earth. Once a year they cooked and ate a wild, natural, hallucinatory mushroom soup to celebrate their sacramental solstice. That celebration was right around the corner. The MEP didn't kill anybody unless they had to and didn't talk about it when they did.

Wearing a black and green plaid flannel shirt, Tripper stood in a wide stance at the base of a coastal redwood tree in the center of the grove amid a still healthy fern forest. Wiping callused hands on faded blue jeans, she adjusted her posture, making sure the heavy, steel-toed work boots dug into the soft moist ground that never dries completely because of dense fog and ocean mist. Grounded and balancing her tall frame, Tripper connected with Mother Earth, her creator, and extended her arms as far as she could reach around the rough bark of one of the world's tallest trees.

An average redwood lives for 500 to 700 years, although some have been documented at more than 2,000 years old.

Tripper just turned 40.

Tearing up as she placed her cheek against the giant tree's jagged skin, her heart beat against the bark. Extending the best vibes she could muster, Tripper whispered to the tree, knowing the essence of this massive living species felt her embrace and appreciated her affection.

"I love you," Tripper said.

Slowly dropping her arms, she turned and almost walked into Branch, the youngest member of the unit, who immediately got in her face.

"I hear you got a problem with me sending my poems and song lyrics to Charlie."

"Branch, you scared me."

"Charlie loves nature. Charlie loves animals. Charlie loves the universe."

"He's Charles Manson, Branch."

"Charlie wants to be free."

"Can't argue with that."

"Charlie wants to save the environment," Branch said. I'm joining his new group."

"What's the new group?"

"The Order of the Rainbow."

"What's he want from you in return?"

"Avoid sexual intercourse, meat, cigarettes, makeup and movies with violence.»

"You avoid most of that shit already," Tripper said. "And the Mother Earth Patrol is no movie."

"Charlie wants us to help him save the world."

"We want you to help us save the world," Tripper said. "How

172

old are you, Branch?"

"Twenty."

"You really want to be a 21st Century Manson girl?"

"Don't make it sound dirty."

"Dirty is good, Branch. Mother Earth is all about dirt. Evil is bad. Charlie is all about bad."

"You calling me evil?"

"If the Birkenstock fits...."

Tripper walked away, down the trail to the main house where a vegetarian supper stew simmered on the stove in an old fashioned blue and white speckled pot. Eight other women gathered in the communal kitchen, cleaning rifles, making bombs and Molotov cocktails, and attaching trip wires to IED booby traps.

"Almost solstice, Becky," Tripper said.

"Mushroom soup for everybody," Becky said. "Chanterelles and magic schroom buttons are a nice combination. With miso and tofu."

"Don't forget the sherry," Tripper said.

"Psychedelic," Becky said.

"That's exactly the kind of shit Charlie is against," Branch said from the doorway.

"Would you please stop?" Tripper said.

"He took it to the man before you did."

"He organized the killing of nine innocent people we know of and probably more."

"Yeah, but his family wrote 'pig' in blood on the wall because Charlie cared for little living things. He cared for the earth. Charlie's like us, loving animals more than people, because they're more vulnerable than people."

"Look, Branch, granted, none of us care much for most people things. Pigs are radical. We have to look out for them. But more and more people are starting to care about the planet. We need to live together. It's 2017. You can't go around killing what you don't understand. That's why Mother Earth is in the condition she's in."

"The solstice sacrifice needs to take place," Branch said. "One very bad man of our choosing must be sacrificed. A human sacrifice for the summer solstice. Cut out his heart on the altar of the sun."

"Listen, Branch," Tripper said. "You told us about your grand-mother, her being a real Manson girl and all. How your mother fell under his spell as well—Charlie's own daughter. But you're smart and already committed to a good cause with us. Don't get dumb and committed to a locked ward for the rest of your life because of your grandpa."

Branch moved toward Tripper.

"Helter skelter," she said.

Displaying the blue-steel glint of a razor blade she had hidden in her palm, Branch raised the edge to the skin above the bridge of her nose and began to cut. First she drew the blade from right to left and then from left to right, crossing in the middle of the first cut. Bigger than Charlie's, the X started to bleed.

"I'll finish my swastika tomorrow," Branch said.

Giggling, she skipped from the room with blood running into her glassy blue eyes.

VOICES

"There's something wrong with Wally," Rose said.

Motionless on the pull-out bed in the van, he sat frozen in full lotus like a carved stone Buddha. The inside of Wally's head felt like a demolition derby was underway with shrill voices crashing, smashing, screeching, squealing, banging and careening off the sides of his cranium. Wally could not move or speak.

"I said there is something wrong with Wally," Rose said.

"So what else is new?" Jesús said.

Walking to Wally's side, Jesús touched his shoulder. Wally's soaked T-shirt and body felt cold. Although Wally looked like he was sitting still, his body quivered as if a constant internal electric buzz ran through him from head to toe.

"Wally," Jesús said. "C'mon, man, snap out of it."

War had broken out in Wally's head where Syrah no longer had the place to herself. Now Syrah heard voices, firm, challenging voices she had never before encountered. Rational yet threatening, the voices tried to persuade her to leave Wally so he could live a happy life and to leave the world alone rather than creating more victims for Wally to kill and kill and kill again. All tried and failed to convince Syrah to live in peace, to practice witchcraft for the benefit of others.

Then the discussion stopped.

Wally came to.

"We're in trouble," he said.

"Fucking A," Syrah said.

When the voice in your head starts hearing voices in her head, there's nowhere to go but down.

SNAKE EYES

AFTER passing out drunk during Father Fresa's wake, Gagliardi's snores blasted from his open mouth in a burst of spit and halitosis. Two of his henchmen carried him from the VFW social hall where they weren't welcome but showed up just the same, armed and dangerous just to keep an eye on the proceedings in case anybody got any ideas Gagliardi wasn't still in charge.

By the time the men got him home, pulled off his boots and pushed him face-forward and clothed onto the bed, the snake had slowly made its way up the leather of Gagliardi's left boot under his pant leg and curled around his calf where it rested snug against the fabric of his sock.

Many miles north, Jesús Zarate slept, shifting restlessly in bed in his room at the Pied Piper Motel in Stinson Beach, where the crew checked in for a few well-deserved days of rest and relaxation before digging deeper into their Northern California pilgrimage.

Happy now, Wally wanted to see a great white shark in its natural habitat. Wallace wanted to think and tune up his bike. Rose needed sunshine on the wide stretch of beige beach. And Syrah needed to replenish her venom now that she was being ganged up on by mysterious powers she worried were greater than she.

Wallace and Wally had not talked about their relationship since the genetic bomb dropped at the pier. They liked to think they had all the time in the world, but time moves forward not backward as they played too fast with fate. In this pack, everybody ran the risk of destruction. Everybody could come too close to dying. Everybody knew somebody would.

In his dream Jesús saw a snake moving up Detective Gagliardi's leg, past scars of a recent knee replacement, to an upper thigh dappled with cellulite that spread to his buttocks. The snake rooted through the cop's nest of pubic hair and hesitated, attracted by dank warmth in the foul-smelling recess of his rectum. Stretching to full size, the viper moved past Gagliardi's belly button, splitting soft chest hair as it slid to his neck, over his cheek and into his wide open mouth.

A sleeping man would normally sense the pressure and air blockage of a snake crawling into his mouth and slithering down his throat. An unconscious drunken slob such as Gagliardi, however, merely coughed and choked briefly as he took short gagging breaths until the snake burrowed into his body and prepared to strike from the inside. The viper's first bite woke Gagliardi with the thought of hot needles digging into his chest. The snake's second charged strike paralyzed his esophagus. The third sting pierced the diaphragm. A small stream of blood trickled from Gagliardi's mouth and pooled in a quarter-sized circle on his pillow. The snake went to sleep in the cop's stomach and found its way out by morning.

Jesús awoke refreshed, the dream history, weight lifted from his conscience. He would check for Gagliardi's obituary when he had a chance to go online. No rush, though. Jesús knew Gagliardi was dead and that his spiritual power to do good against evil was growing.

When justified, revenge tasted sweet.

Violence is not the answer—until it is.

NIRVANA

A FTER two days at the Pied Piper the entourage saddled up and headed north on an idyllic ride through nature's coastal edginess. Having a good time despite some severely disordered dysfunction, this odd band tried their best to lighten up, blowing horns and pointing whenever something special caught their attention.

Stopping outside Bolinas in a roadhouse bar for grilled oysters with salt, hot sauce and lime, they relaxed and drank strong craft brew beers. Playing 80s oldies on the juke box, everybody danced with Rose and treated her with more respect than she had ever known.

When Rose and Jesús went to the bathroom, Wallace reached across the table and placed his right hand on top of Wally's right hand.

"If I ever found you, I was going to kill you," he said. "For running out on my mother and me."

"I...," Wally said.

"Just listen," Wallace said. "But you didn't know. I'm glad fate brought us together. As fucked up as we both are. I'm glad you're here."

Wally placed his left hand on top of Wallace's right.

"You can say that again, son," he said.

Both men were still laughing and had ordered another round of beers when Jesús and Rose returned.

"We miss something?" Rose said.

"Inside joke," Wally said.

"They're the best kind," Jesús said. "That means you belong to something."

Cali's most notorious fugitives pulled into camp on the outskirts of Mendocino by nightfall.

"My buddy Skeeter's father willed him this cabin right before Skeeter joined the Army," Wallace said. "When he died in a Taliban firefight he willed it to me as part of our pact."

"What did you promise him in case you died in combat first?" Wally asked.

"My motorcycle."

"Now you have them both," Rose said. "Make the best of a bad situation."

"We should all do that."

Taking Rose by the hand, Wallace walked to the front door.

"At least you and I haven't killed anybody yet," he said.

"We're both targets," Rose said.

"As long as we have drugs and alcohol we're deadly," Wallace said.

"You kill anybody in the war, Wallace?" Rose said.

"Men, women and children," he said. "It's just the way it went down, sometimes by accident, sometimes on purpose. Sometimes without knowing who I killed or caring, I killed anything and everybody who could kill me—dogs and cats, too. I even killed trees."

Rose listened with a mix of pity and revulsion.

"That answer your question?" Wallace said.

Clutching Animal's leather-fringed bag to her chest, Rose stood by as Wallace unlocked and opened the door. Other than a minor mildew smell, the spotless cabin shined with knotty pine walls and redwood beams. A stone fireplace rose almost to the ceiling and yawned big enough to stand in and cook. An antique china closet sparkled in the light of the kerosene lamps they lit throughout the lodge. Three bedrooms, a bathroom with a shower and tub, a full kitchen, dining room and large living room completed what comprised luxurious quarters for such a wandering band of misfits.

Taking in the atmosphere, Wally sensed harmony for the first time in years. Maybe he could talk Syrah into a truce, a long drawn-out cease-fire that could lead to peace of mind. That's all Wally ever wanted—peace of mind. But a peace treaty with Syrah was so much easier said than done.

"Nice place, man," Jesús said. "You sure it's okay we stay?"

"Long as you like. We can rally from here. This is where I make my stand. I never thought I could handle living here. Now I have no choice, like it was meant to be. Stranger things have happened."

"And we're as strange as they come," Syrah said.

"I'm going salmon fishing," Wally said. "I saw nets and poles on the back porch."

"Sorry, Wally," Wallace said. "No go."

His feelings hurt, Wally looked at the floor.

"It's not your fault," Wallace said. "River salmon fishing is banned. Salmon all but don't exist in the once clean, once cold rivers. People killed their habitat. Logging, road cuts, clear-cuts, off-road vehicles, poorly planned railroads and, above all, people wiped out the salmon."

"I'll just go for a walk," Wally said.

"Don't stray too far," Wallace said. "No telling what other kind of life still does exist in this forest, and they're probably pretty pissed at people, too."

Jesús walked to the polished, mahogany gun cabinet that took up a corner of the living room.

"All quality merchandise," he said. "Looks like your partner was ready for anything."

"Nobody's ever really ready for anything," Wallace said.

"Sorry, man," Jesús said. "I don't mean to upset you."

"No need to apologize. Sometimes nothing can save you."

The scream tore through the air, high-pitched and frantic. Scrambling out the doors, Jesús out the front and Wallace out the back, they heard a second desperate cry for help. About 50 yards into the tree line, they spotted Wally hanging upside down about six feet above the ground, secured by a tight snare that hooked his ankle. Wallace quickly detected the brown bungee cord that secured the trap and cut it easily with his knife. Wally dropped without injury into soft leaves and underbrush.

"That's not Skeeter's booby trap," Wallace said. "Skeeter's trap would have taken off his leg."

"Amateur?" Jesús asked.

"Looks like it," Wallace said.

"Probably some kids," Rose said.

"Or somebody who wants to hunt us," Wallace said. "I got first watch. Everybody get some sleep."

Two hours later Wallace stood beside a cheap headstone with the word "WAR" carved in the center. Mindful of his surroundings as the world spun out of control, he fought the urge to say a childhood prayer because he knew praying wouldn't do anybody any good.

"Rest in peace, Skeeter," he said. "I'm sorry I let you down."

TRIPPER TIME

SIPPING hot chamomile tea, her legs pulled under her and covered with a blue and pink crocheted afghan, Tripper watched 60s motorcycle movies on TV.

Born in 1977, she considered herself a child of the 60s. Her birthday was Earth Day. Now six months after swearing off hallucinogens, Tripper felt cleaner, more mentally sound than ever. Decades of mostly organic mescaline trips—peppered with the occasional LSD adventure followed more recently by the rare pop of Molly—had opened her mind, and on more than one occasion scared her when she lost sense of self and drifted into a vast red mental void where she worried she might remain. But she always slipped back to herself. Losing track of who she was and what she stood for was not her bag. Branch worried her for exactly those reasons. An Ecstasy and Adderall freak, aided by super strains of dynamite bud, the kid became more and more unpredictable each day. A year in the squad had honed her operational skills but her social skills deteriorated significantly, interfering with her ability to get along with the other women who, by and large, behaved with strict discipline and surprisingly good humor.

Almost none of the women still used drugs. Those who did stayed with cannabis edibles, lotions and potions. Wine was fine, and they considered the yearly mushroom soup supper to be sacramental and holy. Everybody seemed thankful they had escaped the clutches of hard drug use including heroin, meth, pain pills, antidepressants and organized Christianity.

Wicca was nice, but their own individually personalized brand of natural worship meant more as they planned together and took direct action against the real enemy of the people—developers and their lackeys who did as they were told and never questioned their masters' bidding.

Sensing a presence behind her, Tripper looked over her shoulder.

"Hi, Branch," she said.

"Why don't you like me?" Branch said.

"You want the truth?"

Branch flinched.

"You really don't like me?"

Tripper kicked off the afghan and stood to full height.

"You will soon crash and burn, sister. You will take one or more of us with you unless you smarten up. And I mean soon. I will not allow that to happen. We accepted you into the unit because of your nerve. We agreed you would learn, get tougher. You now carry more weakness than strength. We can't carry you any longer. You are the weak link."

"You're fucking voting me off the island."

"Get real, Branch. This is not reality television. We don't have television here, remember? You do more harm than good. The dope is eating into your brain, making you paranoid and aggressive toward people who love you. Last week you called Becky that one horrible word a woman cannot call another woman. You have one week. We will help if we can. But you must ultimately go it alone. Get straight or go."

Tripper caught Branch's wrist before the Gerber fighting knife came out.

"Did I say you have a week?" Tripper asked. "You just lost a day because of your volatility. You have six days."

Becky stuck her head through the crystal beaded curtain that separated rooms.

"Everybody cool here?" she asked.

Branch cursed, calling Becky that awful name again.

"Five days," Tripper said.

SEPPUKU

"**Y**OU said we haven't killed anybody yet," Rose said.
"Yeah, and you said we're targets," Wallace said.
"You think we might be dead already?" she asked.
"And we don't even know it," he said.
"You're scaring me, Wallace."
"No more than I'm scaring myself."
Rose reached for Wallace. They held each other.
"I don't know what to do to get better," she said.
"I don't either," he said.
"We're goners."
"Yeah."
Rose laid out six lines of meth. Wallace poured whiskey. Three lines for her. Three lines for him. One shot apiece.
Feeling worn out and embarrassed, they just stared at their favorite intoxicants.
"Want to just go for a long walk instead?" Wallace asked.
"Sounds nice."
Wallace and Rose held hands, walking slowly for miles deep into the forest. Feeling a little better from the fresh air, Wallace started to relax. Stumbling through leaves and underbrush, Rose almost fell, regained her balance and walked slower, a mess of emotion and fear. Getting tired quickly, she slipped and twisted her ankle. On the ground she started to cry.
When Wallace moved to Rose's side and lifted her to her feet, he took one hop step backward to regain his balance when the earth

opened and swallowed them. Branch watched from the lower limbs of a redwood, tracking them as they came her way and fell. The pit covered with sticks and leaves worked too easily.

Even standing on Wallace's shoulders, Rose failed to find a foothold to climb out. As heavy as Wallace was on Rose's shoulders, he, too, missed any way to claw or jump his way to freedom. Trapped amid soft mud and small stones, their minds raced.

"Jesús will find us," Rose said.

"We walked for two hours. We're too far in," Wallace said. "Nobody will hear us."

As Wallace looked up to the edge, a piece of typing paper appeared in the air and fluttered to the ground. A cooking pot, tied by the handles with thick white twine, lowered slowly. Two honey protein bars and two bags of unsalted peanuts followed, ricocheting against the dirt walls on their way down.

"Who are you?" Wallace yelled. "Show your face."

A black balaclava-clad head appeared and quickly disappeared over the edge.

Rose picked up the typing paper and read the communiqué out loud.

"You are prisoners of the Mother Earth Patrol for your crimes against nature. You will be fed daily. Drinking and bathing water will be provided. Use the soup pot for personal waste. We will retrieve and empty the pot daily. We urge you to show remorse for your crimes. Love your mother."

When Rose finished, a steady flow of cold spring water poured from above as she and Wallace leaped out of the way. The shower's intent dawned on Wallace and Rose at the same time.

"There goes our drinking and bath water," Wallace said.

Rose tried to keep from falling apart.

"You know what cold turkey is, don't you, Wallace?" she said.

FRUIT OF THE VINE

"NOT all fine wine is snob wine, Wally," Jesús said. "You need to make peace with the wine, be one with the wine."

From where they sat in two green Adirondack chairs set up on the grass overlooking the bluff, they watched creamy ocean waves crashing against the rocks below. A half-full bottle of pinot noir rested at the center of a French oak wine barrel that served as a table. Crumbles of raw sheep milk cheese and fresh apple slices on napkins gave the scene a greeting card look. The winery clearly appealed to the bourgeoisie.

"I'm partial to pinot," Wally said, trying to play the game.

"There you go," Jesús said.

Presumptuous to a fault, the winery and vineyard still provided respite from their trek and increasing problems.

"Wallace and Rose would love this," Wally said. "I wonder where they went."

"They have some issues to work out," Jesús said.

Wherever they were, they hadn't come home last night and weren't around when he and Wally awakened. One reason Jesús decided to take Wally wine tasting was to get his mind off their absence.

"Get your nose into your glass, Wally," Jesús said. "What do you sense?"

Wally played along now, having fun for a change.

"Moderately dim, boxing bruise color. Extremely modest with a red, bashful nose, lazily revealing scrumptious colors of blackberry tarts, midnight preserves and cowboy boot leather on toast. A mouth-filling center filled with chocolate éclairs wrapped in humble tannins finishing with an upshot of burdened yet tasty savory fruit."

Jesús couldn't stop laughing.

"You next," Wally said.

Jesús plunged his nose into his wine glass.

"A double bubble gum start to a Mexican hat dance finish," Jesús said. "Tones of blustery Pacific whale blubber compounded by a rusty gate gash from a rustier nail that bleeds into your strawberry shortcake and makes you worry your hair might burst into flames."

Wally stopped laughing.

"See, even you can't leave the misery alone," he said.

Jesús looked puzzled.

"Even when we're having fun and goofing on the wine snobs, you had to mention blood. You had to bring back strawberry memories of happier times when we believed justice would prevail and the bad men killed Father Fresa."

"I thought you were going to try to have a good time."

"And remember when Michael Jackson's hair caught fire?"

"The Pepsi commercial," Jesús said. "Michael bums you out, too."

"Even though he's dead he hurt all those children," Wally said. "They have to live the rest of their lives with his dirty fingerprints all over them."

"You going to drink that?" Jesús asked, pointing to Wally's wine.

"No."

Jesús threw his wine back, picked up Wally's glass and threw his back as well.

"Let's go," he said. "Time to find the missing persons."

"Are you gentlemen finished?" asked a smart-looking young woman wearing a crisp white apron.

"Yeah," Jesús said, dropping a 20-dollar tip on the barrel.

"Come again soon," she said, picking up the tip. "Ask for me. I'll get you a discount."

"What's your name?" Wally asked.

"Branch," she said with a wink.

"Later, Branch," Jesús said.

Shoving the money into the left pocket of her apron, Branch didn't know how lucky she was. In her right pocket small claws tightened. A curled tail juiced with poison grew tense. Always ready to strike, Regalo waited.

Few gifts have the ability to wait and watch the way a scorpion can. With 12 pair of alert eyes following this young woman who gave off an air of suffering, the scorpion knew well the potential obstacles he and his master were up against.

Time was on his side.

Regalo rested.

The best gifts are the most useful gifts.

SYRAH SMILES

PLEASE just listen, Wally. Just in case you think I'm having a good time, life is no lark in the park when you're a voice in somebody's head. I didn't ask for this ride. Nobody thinks I have any rights, but I do. Like you, I have the right to remain silent. Ha ha, that's a joke. But I'm not shutting up for anybody. I plan to get worse. I'm real sick of hearing you whining all the time about how bad life has treated you. If you were stronger you could win. If you took your meds, you could really win. Shut me down for good. Keep me quiet. Gag me. Kill me. I'm glad your hippie mother died. She was way too pushy. Getting little baby Wally to take his pills every day, go to work at that fucking winery, get treatment for mental illness and embrace touchy feely therapy. And then what happened? They locked you up in the rubber room until doctors revealed how very bright, very sensitive and very psychotic you are. These know-it-alls we're travelling with should see how sensitive you are when you start waving around that corkscrew of yours. Who the fuck do they think they are? Jesús of Santa Maria is the worst. Control freak. And I know he has something to do with sending those voices into my head. Sending voices into a voice's head that operates in somebody else's head? That's scary shit, out of line and completely inappropriate. How does he do that? I got to find an ally, a kindred spirit voice in my head to battle those alien voices if they attack me again. Some of them are yelling at me in Spanish. Get this straight, Wally. You're the chief head case here. But leave it to me. I'll take care of everybody one night when they're asleep so I can have you all to myself.

Settle down. Drink nothing but the best blood red Syrah we can find. Here's to us, dearest Wally, my love. Here's to blood red syrah.

THE VIPER DID HIS WORK

"**G**AGLIARDI'S gone," Jesús said. "I just got a text from a maintenance man at the newspaper."

Anger braided Wally's emotions as echoes of thumping bongos started and stopped in his head. Surf guitar riffs tore through his brain cells while he hallucinated a yellow bird flying madly around a cage, banging off wire walls and losing feathers in the chaos. Syrah's voice sounded like wine glasses smashing.

"That's not fair," Syrah said. "The strawberry priest was Wally's friend. You owed Wally revenge. Wally earned the right of first reprisal."

"It's best this way, Wally," Jesús said. "It's good for you, too, Syrah."

"How did he die?" Wally asked.

"Snake bit him," Jesús said. "Just a fluke."

Defeated and drained, Wally pouted. Destiny denied him his due. Nothing went Wally's way.

"We have more serious problems, Wally" Jesús said. "Where can Rose and Wallace be? This is Wallace's refuge. This was supposed to be his sanctuary."

"Should we search?"

"We're way out of our league up here, man" Jesús said. "I don't know anybody to call for help."

Exhausted now and nodding off on the couch, Wally's nightmares came fast. Jesús let him whimper and flail but didn't try to wake him. For some reason, he, too, was feeling sleepy and settled into an overstuffed arm chair, stretching out his long legs, crossing his green cowboy boots at the ankles. Soon he was asleep.

In the depth of his trance, super saint Jesús Malverde appeared in a fog.

"You insulted me, mijo," Malverde said. "Telling your troubled friend you did not know who to call for help."

"I'm sorry."

"You also do not understand why your mother disappeared."

"I do not."

"She will surface when she is ready."

"I'm worried about my friends."

"You are quick to call them friends. Is that not hasty?"

From where he stood as if hovering on a cloud, Jesús Zarate looked down and saw his own body. Alone and feeling fragile, instead of increasing his strength a wave of weakness struck, hinting trouble traveling his way.

"In case you haven't noticed, Regalo is gone, too," Malverde said. "On a mission."

"Regalo has a mind of his own," Jesús said. "The viper also did his work."

"So did the coyote," Malverde said.

Jesús tensed.

"A little over the top, don't you think?" he said.

"A coyote must hunt," Malverde said. "Evolution depends on predation."

"Spoken like the true Mexican Robin Hood," Jesús said.

Malverde laughed.

"We take from the rich and give to the poor," he said.

"The search for truth continues," Jesús said.

"As sure as you are my blood," Malverde said.

SACRIFICE

BORN on the Spahn Ranch in Los Angeles County where a few Manson family scouts stayed in the spring of 1969, a month or so before Charlie moved in, Branch's mother took her first newborn breath of fresh air as cheering, naked family members surrounded her birth.

Dancing like wood nymphs, men, women and children circled Branch's grandmother who stretched out on a dirty bare mattress on the bunkhouse floor. Chanting song lyrics from the British invasion and other freaky deaky psychedelic gobbledygook, they cast white magic spells, saving black magic hexes for later. Few people have heard about the Manson babies, but they exist, drained of public heritage and pumped up with Manson DNA. Branch's mother considered herself a proud holder of such succession, a keeper of the mysticism that filled Charlie and made her a genome match to menace. Nobody ever called Manson "Grandpa" to his face.

Branch's mother made her promise not to tell. But one day she planned to do just that, to visit and tell Charlie to his face how much she loved who she was and who he was and what he taught her through the mental telepathy they shared. She almost couldn't wait to explain her plans to further their revolution by burning California to save it.

American soldiers once held high their Zippos when they torched peasant huts in Vietnam. Branch hoarded railroad flares, including boxes she stole from an 18-wheeler parked outside a truck stop diner in Ukiah. With an incendiary personality and capable of anything, Branch sure got around.

Sucking a fat white piece of teriyaki bean curd into her mouth at dinner that night, Branch swallowed and calmly said she had an announcement to make.

"We have two captives," she said.

Tripper dropped her chop sticks.

"Explain," she said.

"I've been tracking them ever since I spotted them buying ice at the general store. They're staying at the dead soldier's lodge. Four targets altogether. But the two I got are a couple."

"A couple of what?" Tripper asked.

"A couple of POWs," she said. "Prisoners of women."

The other women sat silently at the long dining table.

"We'll weaken them for two weeks. Play with them. Tease them. Taunt them. Then we use biker man as our human sacrifice. The damsel can serve as our sex slave."

"The Mother Earth Patrol is about discipline and the land. Your savage shit is psycho shit," Tripper said. "We are a crack insurgent team of eco-warriors. We don't make human sacrifices. We don't take slaves. We don't disrespect ourselves with barbarism. And we do not play with anybody."

Branch's expression hardened. Her voice got dreamy. She fingered the deer bone handle of the knife she wore on her waist in a rawhide sheath tied to her thigh with a leather cord.

"When they pass out in the pit we hogtie them and bring them here. We'll deprogram her. As for him, I know how to butcher. I saw it on YouTube. A divine offering of a still beating heart to the goddesses will strengthen us for the coming war."

Spinning on her heel, Branch turned and skipped from the dining room like an excited 11-year-old on her way to the playground. The women did not speak. A tear slowly rolled down Becky's cheek and dropped on the red and white checked plastic table cloth.

"Anybody want to smoke a joint?" Tripper asked.

WALLY SPEAKS

To whom it may concern: All I ever wanted to be was happy. I never wanted to hurt anybody. But my head took off on a bad trip all by itself. Syrah moved in when I least expected company. Now I can't control her. I'm afraid. She makes an ass out of me all the time. She pushes me. I'm worried I'll let her down and won't be there to protect her when the time comes. But who protects me? She says she does, but somebody always dies in the process. I just want peace. That's why I like Japanese food and want to be a Buddha. That's why I meditate and eat minute rice on the road. Wouldn't it be nice to sit on the beach drinking sake rice wine just for sake's sake? Say that out loud. Sake for sake's sake. Sake for sake's sake. Haha. Been enlightened yet? I have. I'm sorry. I haven't been enlightened yet and probably never will reach that peak on the mountain. I heard a story once about a holy man who was born with an extraordinary golden screw for a belly button. Stretched out on a mountain peak, contemplating his navel and awaiting enlightenment, one day the sky opened and a giant golden screwdriver slowly lowered from the clouds. The screwdriver came closer and closer to his belly, finally reaching his navel where it made contact and started to turn. The screwdriver turned and turned in his belly button, finally removing the golden screw, lifting it heavenward where screw and screwdriver disappeared into the clouds. Inspired and eager to share his moment of truth, the monk jumped up to race to the monastery. You know what happened? You know what happened? His ass fell off. The moral of the story is so simple: Don't let your ass fall off. Mine feels like it's ready to drop. Syrah's holding the screwdriver and I'm just waiting to fall apart. How can I stop her? What power do I have? My mother wouldn't let my ass fall off. She held me together. Now what? Now what?

PIT STOP

TREMBLING involuntarily, Wallace had to admit he was scared. Sweating and aching, Rose's bones hurt. Wallace visualized Arabs. Rose called for her mother.

"The sun is shining in my face and I have goose bumps like I'm freezing," she said.

"I forgot your name," Wallace said.

In their shared cramped space little room existed for his boozy delirium tremors and her withdrawal from opioids. The muddy pit could not accommodate the symptoms for one emergency, let alone two. But after three days and nights alone, their personal expressions of alcoholism and narcotic addiction seethed hot and heavy.

"I have to get out of here," Rose said.

Drawing each word out dramatically in high-pitched sobs, she clawed at the dirt sides of what felt more and more like a grave. Trying to find a foothold, she slipped once, twice and three times before giving up.

"Goddammit, knock it off," Wallace snapped. "I just want some sleep."

"You've been sleeping for hours already," Rose said. "Big biker combat vet jerk-off. What good are you? Get me out of here."

Grabbing Rose by the shoulders he threw her to his left side.

"Watch out," he yelled.

Rose slammed headfirst into the side of the hole.

"There," Wallace screamed. "Arabs."

Rose became afraid—and not of any Arabs.

"Wallace," she said. "There are no Arabs."

"My heart is racing," he said. "I feel like it's coming through my chest."

Muscles in Rose's left thigh cramped and she grabbed for her leg. Another cramp hit her right thigh as she cried out hysterically and hit the ground. Now Wallace cried out when the seizure hit. Shaking violently, an electric storm in his brain told him he had been there before. Rose lay helpless, deep in her own pain, petrified of whatever horror might come next. He couldn't hear. He couldn't see. She reached for him. He pulled away. Curling into a fetal position he questioned the abyss.

"Why, why, why?" Wallace said.

"Please, Wallace, please," Rose said.

Begging for help, Rose passed out.

Wallace thought he died.

Overhead Branch threw two granola bars and two bags of honey roasted peanuts into the pit. A cold spring water shower from a plastic bottle followed. So did a rusted straight razor with a plastic handle, recently sharpened just in case somebody needed to kill somebody or slit his or her wrists in a fit of panic.

Beneath a clump of leaves, 12 eyes watched to see which way Branch would try to depart. Time was running out—for her, and for everybody else. A viper glided unseen by the toe of her jungle boot. A coyote crouched in the timber cover. Spirits prepared to spend another night waiting for the bells of hell to sound their chilling alarm.

PIPELINE PANIC

"**W**HERE are they, Branch?" Tripper asked. "Tell me now."

Three days had passed. Branch still refused to provide the location of her pit captives. Tripper worried police would somehow start searching and all her planning and hard work for the upcoming operation would be fruitless.

"We hit the gas pipeline construction site in two days," Tripper said. "We need all hands on deck, focused and ready for action."

"My prisoners are more important than the pipeline," Branch said. "Human sacrifice will get people's attention more than dynamite ever could. I agree with you that the sex slave role for the girl is not smart. We'll shrink their heads. How about that, ladies? Two shrunken heads for our cause."

"What exactly is your cause, Branch?"

At this stage of her breakdown Branch truly didn't know.

The team met the night before and voted unanimously to expel Branch from the group. Unity is nice when you have it. But Branch was falling apart fast and would take everybody with her.

Tripper stepped to her young adversary.

"A branch is only as strong as its weakest twig," she said. "You understand what I'm saying?"

Holding back tears of rage, Branch backed out of the room, never for a moment taking her eyes off Tripper.

When Tripper first met Branch the young woman was 19, an ex-convict shoplifter working at a winery serving up paired finger foods to go with boutique chardonnay. Tripper noticed the "Love

Your Mother" bumper sticker on her used Honda Accord and asked what Branch thought about the proposed pipeline.

"Somebody should blow that fucker sky high," Branch said.

The kid moved into camp the following week.

Other women came to Tripper from the patchwork people quilt that made up any and every part of Northern California. Disenchanted with personal lives and the unraveling natural world around them, they rejected all violence other than self-defense—which still gave them a lot of room to move. Tripper made sense to them when she spoke about standing strong for Mother Earth as women because mostly men took out their viciousness on her. The women understood all too well harassment and assault by men. Three had served in the military. Two had worked in the entertainment industry. Becky had been a police officer and one had run a dojo—a natural Tripper tapped to serve as unit martial arts training officer.

Tripper had worked for the Chevron oil company—which bought the Unocal oil company that killed old town Avila Beach with a toxic underground lake discovered in 1989 and comprised of more than 22,000 gallons of pipeline-leaked crude oil, diesel fuel and gasoline from a 100-year-old tank farm with no corporate conscience.

The Unocal bosses knew about the leaks as far back as 1977 but never bothered to mention them. They were more concerned about piping the product to ships that docked and pushed off from the local piers. Oil pipeline bosses never really say they're sorry—even when they pay out $200 million in clean-up and damages.

Unocal admitted fault for leaking as much as 8.5 million gallons of petroleum thinner into the ocean and ground water from pipes at its Guadalupe oil field, about 15 miles south of Avila.

Nice people, huh?

Tripper's then-husband Chuck thought so.

Boasting that oil-induced gentrification would improve property values and send the riffraff who lived in trailers packing, Chuck defended the oil company, refusing to accept any personal responsibility for the toxic spills. He and his bloated plutocratic buddies laughed at the trouble they caused and planned to capitalize on the aftermath. Buying up cheap poisoned property, they cared nothing about the land. The destroyed town rebuilt, but the beautiful people took over. Chevron proposed turning the tank farm into a luxury resort.

During a late night spat in 2013, Barbara Ann—the name by which Tripper was known in those days—argued how much better off the people of Avila were with the old town than the new town. Tripper told her husband, Chuck, a Chevron vice president of procurement, that the Charles Shaw "Two-Buck Chuck" wine Trader Joe's supermarket carried, had more class than he did.

"You're slimier than a fresh oil slick," she said.

Winding up and telegraphing his intent, Chuck's open-hander caught Barbara Ann under the chin. Lifting her off her feet, the force of the blow sent her into a side roll across the dining room table. A canine tooth caught the full force of Chuck's Stanford class ring, bouncing as Barbara Ann spit it on the table beside a Waterford crystal wine goblet made in Slovenia.

"Who do you think you are?" Chuck said.

"A woman who cares about the environment," Barbara Ann said. "A woman who will fight for the planet."

Bellowing now, Chuck did an end run around the table like the Cardinal fullback he once was, grabbing her by the hair and dragging her across the floor. Athletic as she was, Barbara Ann could only hang on to her locks and keep breathing during the brutal attack. Conscious breathing made her know she was alive. She knew where she was going. She had been there too many times before.

Chuck first slapped her on their wedding night—said he just reacted. The first closed-fist punch came late on a Saturday night after their first dinner party—said she embarrassed him in front of his bosses. The first two-fisted beating happened after Stanford lost a game to USC.

Chuck kept the laughingly large gold wine spittoon he received as executive-of-the-year beside the fireplace. He would taste chardonnay wine and spit, taste and drool, and never empty the saliva. Just the night before he and his executive friends tasted and spit and tasted and spit, filling the jug with phlegm globs the size of major-league oysters. Barbara Ann long ago vowed to never pour out the foamy yellow sputum and clean the cursed cuspidor.

Only a special kind of slob could invent the kind of punishment she saw coming her way. Chuck either planned to force her to drink, pour the contents over her head, or shove her face into the aging wine spit.

From her position on the ground looking up, all Barbara Ann could do was gnaw on his leg like a dog on a fresh ham hock. Sinking her teeth into the fleshy meat of Chuck's ankle with the force of a bear trap, she sensed bone and kept biting. When Chuck lost his grip on her hair, she rolled to her feet and charged for the den.

High school and college football trophies, squash awards, plastic model oil derricks, framed photographs of Chuck posing with every indecent Republican she could think of, and other mementos of his success lined the floor and the walls.

With the gun cabinet within reach, Barbara Ann focused. Knowing how to shoot and hunt because Chuck made her shoot and hunt on their honeymoon to Wyoming, Barbara Ann grabbed the same antelope rifle that brought down a beauty of a pronghorn the night before they left Laramie for California.

After two weeks of gagging down gamey antelope steaks, burgers, chili and sausage, Barbara Ann gave up eating meat for good—gave up on her marriage, too.

The 25/06 goat gun slipped easily into her hands.

"It's not loaded," Chuck mumbled.

Barbara Ann fired one shot, sending a Winchester Ballistic Silvertip through the stained glass widow over his head. Even barefoot with his ankle gnawed to the bone, Chuck fled like the running back he once was. The Porsche 911 Carrera 4S Coupe engine roared to life in the driveway. Seconds later Barbara saw flashes of custom headlights careen down the road toward the ocean.

Chuck returned three hours later. Barbara Ann heard him pull in, open the front door, and turn on the television. Clutching the rifle, she waited for a full hour, until she got up the nerve to tiptoe into the room to check. Asleep on the red leather couch with his back to her, he posed no danger. Barbara Ann, noticing that his wrapped ankle had received medical attention, wondered just how he explained his wound to the nurses in San Luis Obispo.

Raising the rifle to her shoulder, she sighted him in at about 20 feet and pulled the trigger. The bullet slammed into Chuck's head at the base of his skull, adding a thick coat of jellified crimson and white to the soft red leather furniture. The bullet lodged in the 120-year-old redwood paneled wall made from planks salvaged from a Mendocino shipwreck.

Barbara propped the gun in the corner, poured herself a big glass of pinot noir, and dialed 911.

"I'd like to report an oil spill," she said.

FIRE FURY

SMALL flames turned to big flames then to bigger flames that spread faster than Branch thought they could or would. A nondescript brush trail ignited within seconds of touching the tip of her torch to the ground during a test run a while back near Ojai, where the so-called Piru Fire burned in 2003, reminding New Agers and other area residents that pure wildfire breathed without conscience or philosophical belief.

Fire can kill an acupuncturist as easily as an Orange County stockbroker.

Running and squealing like a toddler chasing orange and black monarch butterflies as squadrons of the beautiful creatures lifted from eucalyptus trees and headed to Mexico, she chased embers and watched an entire orange grove burn. Countless charred black fruit hung from countless smoking trees. Burned and burning oranges stoked her happiness. One day all the people she hated would have nowhere to run after being caught up in her strategically set flash fire.

Seared ahi showed up on every flowery menu in every foodie restaurant on the California coast. Scorched oranges wouldn't go over nearly as well. Time to incinerate California was getting short. Like a crop ready to pick, the time was ripe.

"You want fire pits, you capitalist pigs?" Branch said. "I'll give you fire pits."

Setting California ablaze just dawned on Branch one day at dusk as she watched the sun set over Ventura Beach. With all the

terrorism in the world and concerns rising about rampant gun violence and mass shootings, she realized that California burned every
year without fail and without terrorism. What would happen if a
committed team of committed arsonists planned and carried out
an engaged firebombing of the entire state?

Berserk pandemonium, that's what.

That night she ran away from home, leaving a reiki master
mother and a weak artist father who carved gnomes from tree
branches and sold them to tourists. Saying goodbye to fastidious
parenting for good, Branch took the bus to Mendocino where she
could study the trees and the forest and make a sound plan to burn
them down. Nobody knew the uncertainty that seethed in her
heart. Mother Earth meant the world to Branch but she wanted
more. Branch needed roots and no roots existed. So she decided to
kill whatever grounded existence she could find and call her own.
If she survived, maybe life for everybody would get better. Sound
crazy? Not to Branch.

Mother had survived after Charlie's arrest, trial and imprison-
ment. For many years so had Grandma. Branch's mom and dad dug
the old lady a nice little grave in the backyard beneath a black wal-
nut tree when she passed, as he parents put it, depositing her frail
remains wrapped in a tie-dyed sheet accompanied by a few Buddhist chants and a few old songs from the good old days. Friends
and neighbors excitedly expected other former Manson family
members—hipper, matured and eternally funky—to show for the
interment, but no such luck.

During the 60s, Highway 101 from Los Angeles to San Francisco served as a regular path for Manson family members. Manson
family killer Bobby Beausoleil was even born in nearby Santa Barbara. Branch shook with excitement the day they said goodbye to
grandma. Maybe that's how she got the Charlie bug that turned into
the fire bug. After all, Charlie created fire wherever he went. Charlie inhabited fire. Charlie lived fire. Charlie breathed fire. Charlie
was fire. Branch burned with fire desire.

Before Branch's boyfriend, Russ, died when his bulldozer rolled
over while he was fighting a wildfire near Big Sur, he preached to

her regularly about terrorism by fire.

"One crack squad of 12 fire starters would wreak havoc on the state and the best firefighters in the world," he said. "And we're the best firefighters in the world."

Russ was right. Russ was also dead, mangled in an accident that even the best sometimes cannot avoid. Fate rules despite the best training. But Russ knew how trained revolutionaries could easily put together a radical team drawn from Saudi Arabia, Libya, Iraq, Iran, San Francisco, Seattle or anywhere else and turn the land of milk and honey into one godawful inferno that could easily and relatively quickly incinerate the Golden State.

The idea of "Manson Grrllzz" came to Branch at her 16th birthday party. Somewhere between the carrot cake and the gangster rap karaoke, Branch saw a cloud in the shape of a baby. And she wondered how many Manson descendants like herself were walking around California lost and tattered from what America had become. That night she went online, logging into a new "Smiletime" page and creating a profile she knew would hook teenagers like her who were or wanted to be linked to Charlie's enthusiastic sperm history. "Manson Grrllzz" fire training and self-defense classes would commence as soon as the team recruited Grrlls who fit the bill—Grrlls willing to burn down California and cast all who lived there into the bottomless pit of her personal apocalypse.

After four years, empowered by hundreds of teenage reactionaries who secretly rallied to her cause, a social media circle nothing like cheerleading, Branch wrote songs at night and hoped to have an album ready to record by Christmas. But then she ran away, heading north because her mind was unraveling and Charlie, who she now refused to share with anyone, was calling to her soul.

Tripper had given her good cover to undercut the washed-up old ladies in the Mother Earth Patrol who didn't understand Charlie but were still willing to do what needed to get done to save the planet. Strumming basic guitar chords in her room provided Branch with the solace necessary to muster courage to carry out her plan for Armageddon. She would set Cali on fire all by herself.

"Why does the wind cry gently?" she sang. "When my heart

throbs so glad to be alive? Why does the air die calmly? When my life is a stolen car on overdrive?"

Yeah, Charlie would approve.

The one night she gathered up enough courage to publicly sing her original songs, the audience laughed her off the stage at the Riptide Grill. Russ would have clapped and told her she was great. But all she had was Tripper to hold her and rock her to sleep that night at the compound when failure dominated every second of her life. Vowing to change the world as she knew it, Branch knew the upcoming blood sacrifice—the human sacrifice with emphasis on "man"—would free her, sending a panic cascading through the nation.

"Burn it down," she sang in another song. "Burn it down for tomorrow. Burn it down. Burn it down with no sorrow."

Standing over her prisoners now crawling on all fours in the pit, Branch lit one match after another, firing up a whole book of matches, dropping each one into nothingness as the flame extinguished on the way down.

The man stared back with hollow eyes. The woman moved her head from side to side, blinking as if she had gone blind. Branch scorned their weakness. His bold, yet indecisive deviance sickened her. Her feebleness embarrassed her. Their fawning dependence on each other got them nowhere but trapped deeper in bondage.

Branch dominated, deciding who would live and die.

"Find the heart of the matter," she sang gently. "Watch the failures scatter. Life will soon be fleeting. Hearts will soon stop beating."

WINE DOWN

IN the 85 or so miles between Santa Barbara and Shell Beach, police knew extraordinary problems had come their way. So did the press. Bodies dropping like discarded wine corks, showing up in the oddest circumstances even for California, indicated a troubling pattern developing slowly but surely in an otherwise staid stretch of open road.

Media had no choice but to cover these grisly unhappy hours.

Gruesome wine murders of the lowest order easily chilled the always stodgy grape industry that prefers its lifestyles and moods to be served at room temperature.

As expected, the Wine Buffs Society (WBS) in Santa Barbara issued a typically flat, self-absorbed and defensive press release.

"Vicious rumors designed to harm our business climate and hamper the tourist industry on the Central Coast have run amok. We grieve deeply for those dearly departed whose misfortune has been salaciously sensationalized by media that cannot be trusted to publish real news. Let us also pause for a moment of silence for Santa Maria Mirror Publisher Paige Pennington, who adored the wine we donated to her by the case for years and who is missing and presumed dead. We have faith that if she were here the press would not report these grody deaths attributed to what the fake news media heartlessly calls The Corkscrew Killer.

"As for the alleged killer coyote attack in Shell Beach—outside a low-rent liquor store that sells only our cheaper brands of wine, we might add—we dismiss that accusation as a complete fabrication. The Crushers Motorcycle Club is California's most notorious outlaw gang and is known to engage in grotesque biker on biker mayhem. With them anything is possible, including gang members biting out the throats of other club members. What do you expect from a victim named Animal? These people do not nor will they ever constitute our consumer base.

"As professional wine heads, we continue to welcome you to the Central Coast and invite you to "wine down" with us anytime, anyplace with the "grape expectations" we all deserve.

"Grape lives matter."

SOUTH OF THE BORDER

WITH her feet planted firmly on the floor, seated on a blue velvet couch in an antique-studded house in Culiacan, Mexico, Zita, the town's newest curandero, a psychic healer, straightened her turquoise silk head wrap and prepared for a clairvoyant reading. The seat across the table was empty as Zita directed all her energy at the mental image of her son, Jesús, whose tan, lean face greeted her as soon as she closed her eyes.

Their telepathic mental connection was better than Skype.

"I have missed you, my son," she said.

"And I've been sick with worry about you," he said. "Why did you disappear? Are you all right? Why have you stayed away all these years?"

"You needed time to grow, to expand your power," she said. "You needed to find yourself and your true nature."

"Where are you?"

"Close."

"How close?"

"Close enough to see and hear the coyote."

"The man had two knives," Jesús said. "My training and the volcanic rush of adrenaline helped me defend my friends. They would have died. No coyote did that. I did that."

Flames flickered from a dozen Mexican prayer candles Zita had arranged throughout the room. Heavy red velvet drapes kept out sunlight and unwanted glances from the street. Images of San Judas Tadeo, el Ángel de la Guarda, el Barracho and Santa Muerte danced on the walls while a ceramic bust of Jesús Malverde sat center stage on his shrine.

"You are the coyote," she said.

Malverde burned his presence into Jesús' character.

"Do you feel his power, my son?" Zita asked. "Have you looked in the mirror?"

"Yes," Jesús said.

"Your patrón is always with you," Zita said. "His power is the power of the coyote. His voice is your voice. No difference exists."

"I know," Jesús said. "I am El Coyote. I am Jesús Malverde."

"You have become the man I hoped for," Zita said. "We will speak again soon."

Jesús wanted his mother to stay and help him.

"My friends have disappeared," he said. "Something bad has happened to them."

"They will turn up," she said. "They are safe."

"Will you help me find them?"

"Perhaps they, too, need time—to purify, to cleanse and become whole again."

Jesús knew not to push. His mother's tone soothed him. Confusing riddles no longer surprised him. Family puzzles comforted him, helping him solve problems and better understand his character and his name.

"Yes, they will be all right," he said.

Zita disappeared.

Jesús awoke in the lodge with a start, not knowing for sure if he had actually spoken with his mother or if their conversation had been a dream. Rubbing his eyes, he walked to the kitchen and made a cup of instant coffee. A knock on the door drew his attention through the parted curtain to a woman standing on the back porch holding a salal berry pie.

Jesús slowly opened the door.

"Hi," Tripper said. "Welcome to the neighborhood."

COTTON CANDY HEAD

TRYING to relax, Wally sat on the edge of the cliff, dangling his legs over the edge. Cormorants flew above and below him, providing a delightful feeling that he, too, soared with the birds.

Producing the joint the rock and roll roadie gave him that Wally promised to save for a special occasion, Wally felt the texture of thin Zig Zag cigarette paper as he rolled the fat doobie between his fingers. Sweat trickled from his forehead. Nervousness toyed with his emotions. Wally placed the joint between his lips, struck a wooden stick match and touched the flame to the twisted tip, inhaling as a small flame engulfed the paper.

Dope smoke hit his lungs with force as Wally took a coughing fit that almost sent him over the edge of the cliff. Pounding his chest with the palm of his hand, he tried to control his breathing. Though his eyes watered and sent teardrops down his cheeks, Wally saw the vast spaciousness of the aquamarine sea. Wally took another hit, slower this time, then another.

Three minutes later the first enhanced sensation arrived by special delivery.

The snap of sea gull wings sounded like electric guitar harmony. A second flap of wings provided bass. A third sent Wally swooping through his mind and into a steep glide through conscious thought. The next hit on the joint went down much easier. Slower, smoother, in control, Wally's inhalation produced a full breath that he held and tried to take deep into his lungs. Finally exhaling, he blew a soft stream of smoke seaward.

Wind crawling on his face felt like his head was made of cotton candy wrapped around his nose. A smiling green-scaled mermaid appeared on a rock cluster at the base of the cliff. Combing her hair with a bleached fish bone, she sang a sweet lullaby Wally had not heard since childhood, a song his mother sang to him before he fell asleep. Wally started to laugh. Talking gibberish to himself now, he sang along with the mermaid and saw a tuna wearing sunglasses rise from the sea and dance the hula on the water. The word "effervescent" slid into Wally's head and made him laugh because he had no idea what it meant.

Marijuana nowadays probably burned stronger and purer than ever, Wally thought. Whatever the reason for its potency, Wally dug his new scene. If a couple of tokes on a single stale joint created this kind of high, Wally wanted more. Wally wanted fresh. Wally wanted to grow his own. Maybe that would help—homemade medical marijuana to help reduce his anxiety, clear the crazy voice from his head, and soften the razor sharp edges that turned him into a monster. Wally wanted so much to just chill. Finishing the joint, he reclined with his fingers laced behind his head, watching the clouds roll by. One looked like George Washington. Another reminded him of playful Chinese pandas. Yet another looked like his mother.

Jumping when the joint burned into his fingertips, without even thinking, Wally quickly ate the roach.

That settled it.

Wally would buy a little piece of land in Northern California, stake out a plot, grow his own herb garden, and heal himself. Be good neighbors with Wallace and Rose, bake bread on Sundays, and come over with pot luck dinners to visit as the sun went down.

"Get it, Wally?" he asked himself. "Pot luck?"

Laughing so hard his stomach hurt, Wally eventually settled down, crossed his legs and focused on his breath. Sitting zazen stoned made Wally think he lost his mind. Realizing he didn't care if he found it made Wally start laughing all over again.

Losing your mind can be fun.

MORE PIPELINE PANIC

As difficult as terrorism is to carry out effectively, true patriotism is much harder—especially when you have to start killing people in the name of liberty and justice for all because they really are the enemy.

Each member of the Mother Earth Patrol agreed to kill and die when necessary.

Nobody wanted to take a life or give her own but since most people hated peaceful environmental activists and would attack them at the slightest provocation, these women fighters knew they needed to resort to violence to defend themselves—and, of course, Mother Earth, as planetary self-defenders who merely reacted to real mayhem.

"I'm taking out the first mile of pipeline," Becky said, pointing to the large paper map her teammates had laid out on the dining room table. "The detonator will be located here."

Since dynamite was all they had, dynamite would have to do. It had taken all year to compile the blasting caps and sticks without drawing undue attention. Some they stole, some they exchanged for killer weed they grew, and some they bought legally—purchased as part of their plan to pass themselves off as a legitimate all-female minority small business gold mining operation.

Nobody was mining gold in that part of Mendocino County anymore and little gold, if any, likely existed. So nobody complained when they shared their dreams, stated their goals and laughed at the general store, the local bars or wineries that, "There's gold in them thar hills."

Their innocent cover story worked wonders.

Enough dynamite sat in the storage shed to blow the Golden Gate Bridge if planted properly. With varied expertise and well-rounded knowledge they could sabotage their piece of the pipeline construction site from beginning to end.

Nobody had to die in the process.

Tripper planned to launch the operation when middle-of-the-night security guards fell for the diversion she also planned and mapped out with more dynamite. Blast diversionary dynamite to get the boys running to see what happened. Then set off the main sticks to destroy the target. Out of the line of fire, everybody goes home healthy and happy.

Mission accomplished.

"What if they run back to the target before we get away?" Becky asked.

"That's their problem," Tripper said.

"Copy that," said Mother Jones, the squad's 69-year-old registered nurse, Air Force Vietnam veteran and small arms expert.

"So we're on for tomorrow?" Tripper asked.

"What about Branch?" Becky asked. "Since Charlie died last week, I'm worried she'll break into the lodge, hack us all to death, and write her life story on the knotty pine walls in her own blood."

"You think she'll try to undermine the op?" Mother Jones asked.

"No, I don't," Tripper said. "She's got her problems but she believes in the environment."

"Living Charlie's legacy means carrying out Charlie's legacy," Becky said.

"That's a risk we'll have to take."

"What if she shows up and freaks out?"

"Branch then becomes a liability."

"Will you shoot her?"

"Without thought or malice."

"What would Mother Nature say?"

"What would Charlie say?"

WEED EATERS

WALLY got lost on the way back to the van. Stoned times made for good times so Wally didn't care about rambling and enjoyed the walk to nowhere. Once he realized he had no idea where he was headed, he tried even harder to get there. Succeeding at purposely going nowhere, Wally felt very proud. He tried even harder to lose more of his mind than he had already lost. Finding emptiness became Wally's pure void.

Whoa.

Bad body odor caught his attention as he was trying to imitate an American bald eagle he thought he saw in a sugar pine and swore was really there but didn't care if he imagined the bird because it wore a monocle which Wally considered pompous not to mention the red, white and blue bow tie.

Double whoa.

Just a little paranoid now, Wally smelled gasoline fumes, industrial strength halitosis, sour milk and the overwhelming aroma of marijuana. Powerful and pungent, the scents overpowered his senses and made him gag.

"Freeze, cowboy," the man said. "Do not move."

"You guys aren't for real, are you?" Wally said. "This is, like, guerilla theater or some kind of extreme hip, right?"

The man stepped forward.

"We are the Weed Eaters, white supremacist Christian pot warlords," he said. "I am Commander Fetus."

"Trouble, Wally," Syrah whispered. "You're in real trouble now, mister. The gates to hillbilly heaven are about to open."

Afraid, Wally followed orders and froze, just like the man said.

"You now belong to the master race," Commander Fetus said, producing a roll of silver duct tape from the front pocket of his black Nightstalker fatigue jacket.

Commander Fetus tore off a long piece of tape and slapped it across Wally's mouth. A second piece closed Wally's eyes. A third longer piece bound Wally's wrists. Truck motors roared in Wally's head as his captor marched him 15 paces to the right and pushed him hard with both hands in the middle of his back. The force of the jolt sent Wally sprawling face-first onto the cold metal bed of a pickup truck.

Wally sniffled when his nose started to bleed.

As the truck pulled away, Wally felt a light, warm touch on his thigh. Again he smelled strong body odor and warm breath on his cheek. A voice whispered so quietly he almost couldn't hear the words in his ear or believe them when he did.

"We're alive, Wally," Rose said.

"Not well, but alive," Wallace said.

Regalo rested in Wallace's jacket pocket with six eyes open.

In the cab Commander Fetus talked about the future, excited about going online and buying a new used truck, a big bore blowgun manufactured by Americans for Americans and a new pair of brown suede desert boots. A prisoner of technology even off the grid, he loved shopping online whenever he could connect.

"We'll hold all three of them until we get a ransom," he said. "We're lucky we found them two in that pit."

"Who's paying the ransom?" asked Dread, who wore his hair in thick crusty brown locks that coiled and fell below the middle of his back. A blue Bob Marley tattoo stared from the right side of his neck.

"Those shitheads in the lodge will pay," Commander Fetus said. "They come up here with nice vehicles and a motorcycle. They got money."

"Yeah, now they want to rustle our weed territory," Dread said.

"No way," Commander Fetus said. "As hard as we worked for

our land? No fucking way."

"What about them old girls at the other camp?" Dread asked. "Should we worry about them? They're acting way too nice not to be up to something."

"All they was doing was passing that petition around to stop the pipeline. Bunch of do-gooder liberals is all they are," Commander Fetus said.

"When we going to get our own women, women who do like we tell them and believe everything we say?" Dread asked. "Good Christian birther women who do what they're told."

"As soon as the foreign mail-order catalogues we sent for come into the post office box and we can order our wives," Commander Fetus said. "We're living under God's radar for a reason."

"I want a Russian bride," Dread said. "One named Natasha."

"I'm thinking about a Filipino or two," Commander Fetus said. "As long they're not Mexicans or Mooslems."

"I can't even imagine a Mexican Mooslem," Dread said.

"Don't you kid yourself, boy. They're coming. Mexican Mooslems is crawling across the border as we speak. Al Kidas, too. Mexican Al Kidas. All kind of Al Kidas. Mexican Mooslem Al Kidas. Wanting to snatch up our daughters."

"Lord Heavenly Father, protect us," Dread said.

"I will," Commander Fetus said.

Weed Eaters wanted women they could train like seals, circus seals not Navy SEALS, women who appreciated real men, men like the men who died at the Alamo—American superheroes like the ones they read about in comic books and gun magazines they stole at the general store when they drove into town for supplies.

"This is a great time to be American, huh, Commander Fetus?" said Dread.

"Better than ever, soldier. We got our own army, beaucoup weed, hostages, old- time religion and we're preparing to wake up to the Rapture."

"So where we hide the hostages, Commander Fetus?"

"We're taking them to a rental storage locker by the mall. I lived in apartments worse than that. You did, too. Remember when you lived in that drainage ditch down by the creek?" Commander Fetus said.

"I knew it was time to get up and go to work when the raw sewage flowed over my head in the morning," Dread said. "I got up, too, no matter how hungover I was."

"You were one crack warehouse security guard despite the obstacles you faced in life, young man," Commander Fetus said.

"Thank you, sir," Dread said.

"You all have potential," Commander Fetus said to his men—seven of the most flawed, broken God-fearing marijuana farmers you ever saw. Armed, dangerous and dysfunctional, they had pledged allegiance to Commander Fetus because he believed in them, saved them from themselves and accepted their limitations, no matter how deliriously impaired they were. All the men took an oath to go the limit for their beloved commander, to crash and burn in the name of ignorance, lunacy and a stronger nation.

Of course, Commander Fetus stood ready to sacrifice every last one of these duds in exchange for his own hungry goals. Isolation and failure bewildered him. If plans went well over the next few days, he'd be sitting pretty by Christmas—just him and the new Mrs., whatever race, nationality or ethnicity she happened to be.

Truth be told, he'd settle for a Mexican Mooslem—as long as she unquestioningly accepted Commander Fetus as her personal Savior.

THE END OF THE WORLD

"WOULD you like to sign my petition?" Tripper asked. "Save the forest. Save the planet. Save the world?"

"My mother saved Green Stamps," Jesús said.

Tripper smiled.

"So did mine," she said.

"What'd she get when she cashed them in?"

"Lamps, water glasses, a bathroom scale," she said. "Yours?"

"A chess set. Paints. A wrist watch."

"Cigarette coupons, too," Jesús said. "Remember when smokers peeled them off the back of the packs."

"My mother saved enough in shoe boxes to buy a down payment on a stroke."

"Mine got lung cancer at a discount," Jesús said.

"Good times can turn bad," she said.

"Tell me about it."

"That's why the petition is important," Tripper said. "Even cancer seemed simpler back then. Corporations owned us and we didn't know it. Now Wall Street owns everybody. They don't even want to give you a bathroom scale to measure your obesity or an iron lung to help you take your last breaths. They just rip us off."

"No argument there," Jesús said. "What are the odds the petition will accomplish anything?"

"It shows people care. We get enough signatures we go to our elected officials in Sacramento and in Congress and elsewhere and demand action. They'll listen."

"You really believe that?" he asked.

Tripper stopped talking.

"No, actually I don't."

"Me neither," Jesús said. "You want a cup of tea?"

"That would be awesome."

After two hours of nonstop discussion about everything from cooking oil to not eating shrimp to astrology, Tripper stood to leave.

"You smell smoke?" she asked.

Flames were already rolling down the hill toward the lodge by the time Jesús made it to the low-rider Lincoln and Tripper jumped into her Jeep. Tree limbs ignited overhead and flames licked skyward as they started their vehicles.

"Follow me, "Tripper said.

In her rearview mirror she saw Branch, dressed in a yellow fire proximity suit and racing from one trail to the next, lighting and throwing railroad flares from a compact camouflaged all-terrain vehicle. The flares would burn for 15 minutes, more than enough time to ignite the forest and burn a mark into history until the blackened end of time.

Jesús spotted the maniacal fire starter, too.

Just as Tripper took her eyes off the road for the briefest of seconds, the three-truck mini convoy of Weed Eaters coming toward her pulled to the side of the road. Two men holding assault-type rifles leaped from the vehicles and took cover, taking aim at the approaching enemy.

Out of nowhere a flash of pulsing light appeared behind Tripper and Jesús, briefly blinding the paramilitary men who covered their eyes and struggled to see through their fingers. The strobe radiated so powerfully the Weed Eaters could feel its force, a mutant natural glow used as a weapon against them and their mission.

"Thank you," Jesús said, not sure if his mother or Malverde had anything to do with this dazzling diversion or whether the flashes were just unexplained byproducts of the spreading fire.

Roaring around Tripper's Jeep, Jesús hit the gas and the clutch, shifting hard into third gear, fish-tailing as he kicked up dust and rocks that sent already sloppy commandos tripping over each other to keep their balance.

In the truck bed, Wally felt movement, little legs crawling against the surface of his skin.

Had his captors wrapped the tape completely around his head so it stuck to his hair, unwrapping was pretty much out of the question. But Regalo crawled from Wallace's pocket to Wally, extending one claw to slowly move a pincer beneath the adhesive. Wally had no idea what was on his face but did his best to stay still. Sensing small stirring between his beard stubble and the tape, he slowly worked his jaw back and forth to assist the odd operation. Using its second pincer, Regalo successfully cut through the tape.

Rolling his neck, Wally maneuvered to stick the adhesive end of the tape to the metal truck bed and turned his head to peel the tape from his mouth. Similar dexterity helped him remove the tape across his eyes. Regalo easily scissored through the tape on Wally's wrists.

As Wally undid Rose and Wallace, hysteria erupted from the young lunatic wearing dreadlocks. When Dread slipped and fell on his back, Regalo quickly made his way to the enemy's throat. Using his pincers to dig into Dread's neck, he stung once, twice, three times deep into the muscle marked by Marley's inky beard. Flopping frenzied on his back like a freshly landed salmon, Dread flailed in drastic spasms, bouncing and flip-flopping until his body went limp.

With thumping bongos in his brain, Wally sprang in a flash. Pulling a new corkscrew from his pocket, he plunged the sharp instrument deep into Dread's eyeball. In one smooth motion, he pulled the intact eye from its socket and held it up to the dazzling light the way a jeweler to celebrity stars would inspect a rare diamond engagement ring. Undoing his yucky prize from impalement, Wally struck again, extracting the other blue ball just as easily. Pulling the juicy little globe from the deadly metal coil like a radish from a shish kabob spear, Wally rolled the dripping peeper over the truck bed where it stuck to a paper six pack of Pabst Blue Ribbon beer.

Rose gathered all the adrenaline she could muster and took

a fighting stance like she learned in the women's self-defense class she took during one of her failed in-house rehab stints. Wallace looked on, a mixture of awe and horror in his wide blue eyes. Posturing like a werewolf over a fresh kill, Wally stood to full height.

"Let's go," he commanded Wallace, who dropped from the truck and, as weak as he was, grabbed Dread's semi-automatic rifle, kicking into action like he was back on patrol in Helmand Province, firing in a blind rage on full automatic.

Like father, like son.

New action seized their attention as Regalo scrambled in the dust, turning in agitated circles looking for any unsuspecting enemy to attack. About 15 meters away, Commander Fetus screeched in torment.

At first Wallace, Rose and Wally thought he tripped on a vine and entangled his leg in the growth as he struggled to his feet. The shining head of a great viper told them otherwise as the thick orange and black patterned snake coiled around the leg of Commander Fetus' multi-cam action pants. The faster Commander Fetus ran, the faster the snake gripped and climbed, finally nestling in the hot sweat of its host's groin. Pushing a thick head past the buttons on the crotch, as if out of gratitude or a bonding between two species, the snake found bare skin and kissed Commander Fetus' flesh— digging fangs deep, distributing steaming venom that rushed toward his victim's heart. Mistaking Commander Fetus' limp penis for a cocky garter snake, the viper struck again. The commander's testicles ballooned with poison.

Jesús spun the low-rider in a circle and threw open the door to the three freed prisoners.

"Get in," he said.

Slamming on the brakes, Tripper threw open the Jeep door and opened up with her favorite Mossberg 580A1 Tactical shotgun, knocking two Weed Eaters off their feet after they drew a Bowie knife and Chinese throwing stars, spattering leaky intestines onto a patch of spike moss and a giant chain fir. Slamming the door, she stepped on the gas and saw Wally swoop on the two corpses, brandishing a dripping corkscrew with the ease of a surgeon handling a scalpel.

In less than a minute, whooping and waving his arms, Wally dove into the back seat of Jesús' low-rider Lincoln. With an orchestra of bongo music and surf guitar riffs thrashing in his head, Wally suddenly felt afraid. Trembling, he wept.

For whatever the reason, panic or stupidity, the last of the Weed Eaters lost or dropped his gun and stood his ground in the middle of the dirt road, staring idiotically at impending doom. Tripper's Jeep picked up speed and rolled right through his skinny ass, tearing up flesh and bone with the same ease her four-wheel-drive mountain machine tore up pristine snow drifts in winter and mud bogs in summer.

All that remained on their tail was insanity inspired wildfire that followed them to the main road. Once they hit macadam and cranked up the speed, Jesús led the charge at 100 miles per hour with Tripper following damn near bumper to bumper.

With that, the skies opened and a deluge of rain poured onto the mountain. Flash floods would soon extinguish the fire. Their escape would succeed. They would emerge contemplating terror and an absolutely uncertain future.

Branch's anger would not be contained.

CLEAN AND SOBER

"I NEVER thought I could get off the booze," Wallace said.

"Tell me about it. I was one big walking opioid," Rose said.

"Now you're loaded with vitamins," Wallace said.

"Packed like a B-52 on a bombing mission."

"And I'm guzzling non-alcoholic grape juice."

"Three weeks in a deep open pit will do wonders for sobriety," Rose said.

"You look good, Rose."

"I forgot how handsome you are," she said.

Holding hands, they sat in the hospital discharge lounge waiting for Jesús, who said he'd be there at noon so he'd be there at noon. Nobody likely discovered the Weed Eater corpses yet because of the isolated location. But questions about what happened to Wallace and Rose needed to be answered, and the nurses told them the county detectives would be there by one o'clock.

Any police interrogation would pose major problems, so by then they'd be gone. Too late—as Branch told them as she taunted one day from the edge of the pit—to get a date with Sharon Tate.

"I was ready to give up," Rose said.

"But you didn't. I figured Jesús would find us," Wallace said. "Those Weed Eater fuckers were like something out of a zombie movie. Got the oxygen rushing to my brain, though. I suddenly felt strong, truly righteous."

"I dropped some serious weight in the pit," Rose said.

"My jeans are falling off my hips," Wallace said.

"Amazing how quickly a body can bounce back after a day in the hospital," Rose said.

Rose thought she heard a bark then a howl.

Looking out the window, Wallace said, "There's Jesús."

Hurrying to the shining low-rider that looked no worse for the wear, they shook hands with a grinning Jesús and slid in—Rose in the back and Wallace up front. Genuinely glad to see them, Jesús smiled one of his biggest rarest smiles.

"Welcome home," he said.

"Wherever home happens to be," Rose said.

"First time anybody said that to me," Wallace said.

Driving carefully, Jesús's voice turned grim.

"The women in Tripper's group said we can stay until we get all this crazy shit sorted out," Jesús said. "They expect us to do that soon because they have work to do and are not real keen on having men around or us drawing attention to them."

"I can dig that," Rose said.

"The violence has gone over the top," Jesús said. "Wally is beyond loco and out of control."

Rose leaned forward with her elbows on the seat.

"Did you see him? That corkscrew shit?" she said. "Other than unpredictable bloodthirsty homicidal rampages, though, he's pretty lovable."

"I can relate to that," Wallace said.

"We need to get Wally help," Jesús said. "Then we go our separate ways."

"How do we convince him he's so sick?" Rose asked.

"I want to say 'love,' a whole lot of love," Jesús said. "But Syrah rules and Syrah plays by her rules. Nobody else's."

"She'll disappear under a blast of medication," Wallace said.

"As severely mentally ill as he is, he'll go to jail," Jesús said. "I don't know where or how we can hide him."

"They'll put him in the electric chair," Rose said. "No way, man. Free Wally."

Obeying the speed limit and using turn signals, they covered the distance from the Willits hospital to the Mother Earth Patrol fortress in about 45 minutes where they pulled in the back and covered Tripper's Jeep with dark green jungle netting. Smoke rose from the chimney. Wallace smelled fresh bean soup cooking as soon as he got out of the car. Rose seemed pleased at the notion that women were in charge and she carried some prestige in this crowd.

"I'm not used to being in the majority," she said.

"There he is," Wallace said. "My dear old dad."

Jesús shook his head.

Rose put her hand over her mouth.

Wearing aviator sunglasses with mirror lenses, Wally stood at the front door in a Hawaiian shirt, holding a double margarita in one hand and a bouquet of fresh purple Snapdragons in the other.

INTERVENTION

"A N intervention is like an exorcism with hugs," Jesús said. Wally sang Christmas carols to himself in the kitchen as he placed fresh cupcakes on a platter to carry into the living room to eat with the group's nightly snacks.

"We finish up the night with our coffee and cake then ease into our mental health concerns," Jesús said. "Crying is okay."

"What about Syrah?" Rose asked.

Tripper seemed puzzled.

"Syrah is the killer voice in Wally's head," Jesús said. "The driving force behind his uncontrollable anarchy."

"Typical," Becky said. "Blame it on a woman."

"That's not what I'm saying," Jesús said.

"Then what are you saying?" asked Mother Jones.

"Ultimately Wally is the one and only force of evil here. Wally is male. Ask Wallace over there, seed of Satan and spawn of the Devil that his father has become."

Embarrassed, Wallace conceded.

"That's me, I admit I am, indeed, standing before you in the flesh as the living, breathing product of Wally's loins," he said.

"So everybody in the house is at risk," Tripper said. "We'll have to put Wally under house arrest. Restrain him until we figure out what to do with him."

"What to do with who?" asked Wally.

Rose intercepted him as he tried to balance two dozen cupcakes with extra orange icing and a container of sea salt and caramel non-fat organic frozen yogurt under his arm.

"I found this gallon of ice cream in the refrigerator," he said. "Is it all right if I have some, please?"

Tripper saw why his friends cared so much for him.

"Of course you can, Wally," she said.

After dessert everybody pulled chairs close to Wally's. Tripper threw new wood on the fire and settled in for a long night. Becky shooed the cats and dogs from the room. Jesús felt the presence of his family, soul visitors who showed up whenever and wherever their descendant needed them.

"How are you feeling, Wally?" Jesús said.

"Great, thank you," he said. "I put pretzels in my yogurt."

When everyone smiled, Wally's face contorted as he snarled.

"And I'll stick pretzel sticks up your private parts," Syrah hissed. "You hoes have never seen a real demon before, have you? Bitches rule Hell and you're all invited."

Gasps broke out among the Mother Earth Patrol as Wally's inhabited persona took on a gruff sullen tone of defiance. They marveled how his lip curled like Elvis after a stroke and his facial features turned into another being entirely, not male, not female, but without gender and otherworldly as Syrah addressed the crowd.

"None of you fool me," Syrah said. "You sluts are jealous because I'm the real women's libber here. And you big sacks of testosterone are just namby-pamby wusses, momma's boys, all three of you. Touch me and I slice up your little weenies and stick them on toothpicks for appetizers."

Everybody backed up but Wallace.

"Wally, it's me. It's Wallace. Your son"

Wally's face softened.

"Hi, Wallace," Wally said. "You don't know how good it feels to be with you. Your grandmother would be so proud of you."

"Don't let him bullshit you, Wally," Syrah squawked. "This one percenter outlaw kid of yours is a 100 percenter all right—just like you're 100 percent defective, growing up with that squirrelly earth mother of yours tie-dying your underwear, telling you pop festival bedtime stories, and drinking aftershave lotion at her evening unhappy hour."

When Wallace instinctively stepped toward Syrah, the Mother Earth Patrol interceded and intercepted.

Jesús held up his hand.

"Are you a genuine California peace freak hippie, Wally?" he asked.

Wally furrowed his brow to deeply ponder the question.

"Of course I am, man," he said.

"You don't want to hurt anybody, right?"

"No way."

"A bad personality is living inside you, Wally," Jesús said. "We're trying to help you make life better. Make love, not war, Wally."

"Exactly," Wally said. "Make love, not war. Make love, not war. Make...."

Wally's head fell to his chest as he fell asleep.

"Syrah is regrouping, gaining strength for a final assault," Jesús said. "We can only keep her away so long."

"We?" Rose said.

"My missing witch mother, warlock grandmother and who the hell knows what other dead wizard relatives are stirring the boiling cauldron with my great-grandfather, the Mexican Robin Hood and super saint, Jesús Malverde."

"Never mind," Rose said. "Really, never mind."

Regalo peered from behind a bottle of XXX cheap tequila on the kitchen counter. A beautifully patterned serpent with purple and green overtones burrowed unseen into the woodpile near the stone fireplace. A new fortune teller in Jesús Malverde's hometown lit a match to a votive candle, muttering a gentle prayer to her guide on behalf of her son who would always face danger.

"Cuidado," she said. "Be careful."

BADASS BAIL BONDS

WAKING dazed in his chair, Mendocino County Deputy Sheriff Pete Stiletto, 35, checked his watch and realized he had officially been off duty for two hours. Scratching his balls and standing, he shuffled to the desk in his hunting cabin where he often retreated when on duty. He pulled out an overtime form.

Documenting two hours extra duty—time-and-a-half because it was Sunday—he filed the form in the basket on his desk. He'd submit the extra pay request in the morning when he reported to the sheriff's department for duty.

The flashing red light on his desk phone caught his eye. The voicemail message was short and sweet.

"Deputy, this is bounty hunter Deadeye Jones from Badass Bail Bonds in Oxnard, California. We got a tip on a fugitive biker we're tracking named Animal who was last seen alive on the Central Coast in the vicinity of some pretty bad actors we hear are heading your way. I'm hunting them down for fun and profit. You can make a nice piece of change if you help me grab these desperados."

Going online, Stiletto found Deadeye's Facebook page in 30 seconds—Deadeye taking a selfie of his three-pack abs, Deadeye in bed with two teenage strippers, Deadeye dressed for Halloween as a bleeding Christ on the Cross with real nails pounded into his hands, and a video of Deadeye shooting a pit bull 14 times after claiming the dog was frothing at the mouth and attacked him even though the pup was one month old.

The Associated Press story about the animal cruelty incident said Badass Bail Bonds fired Deadeye but sources said he continued to work under the table. The article also said the froth on the pit bull's mouth was milk suds his owner fed the fearful dog when she gently placed him on the grass at a Jehovah Witness picnic where Deadeye was working security.

A female prison guard commented on the page that Deadeye's nickname intrigued her because it was smoking hot and would he please explain its origin. Deadeye said a senior citizen of Apache descent shot out his eye with a bow and arrow that accidently went off at a powwow where he stopped to try and pick up "Injun chicks."

"My kind of guy," said Stiletto.

Checking the sheriff's website, Stiletto noticed a new press release highlighted in red. The be-on-the-lookout summary alerted California law enforcement to the possibly that slayings of at least four coastal victims in the span of just a few weeks—a wine baron, a movie executive, a real estate broker and an outlaw biker—were related.

Stiletto googled the biker and discovered the dead Animal was the same Animal bail recovery agent Deadeye was hunting. But why did the dumb-ass bounty hunter think "they," whoever they were, were heading his way?

As it turned out, Deadeye had his sources. His ex-wife's girlfriend's sister was working the Shell Beach liquor store that night when she heard a biker and his old lady mention something in a loud argument about a cabin in Mendocino County owned by a dead Afghanistan combat vet. That's when all hell broke loose with a monster coyote attack and a dead Crusher with his windpipe chewed to ribbons.

That's all Deadeye needed to sign on for the pursuit.

If this renegade was coming his way, Stiletto would make the best of it. Quick untraceable cash sounded excellent. Maybe he'd invest in one of the new pot farms in the jurisdiction. After all, he'd been taking bribes to protect illegal plots for over a decade. Why not ramp up a business and brand an identity for himself as a legal entrepreneur like all those Bernie Sanders millennial losers he hated.

Starting up a weed start-up sounded super cool.

Stiletto's cell rang.

"Yeah, yeah, yeah, okay, yeah," he said.

The sheriff wanted Stiletto to stop by the pipeline construction site for a hastily called press conference. Company CEO Col. Jefferson Davis Fields, "Grits" to family and friends, was already at the site, landing by company chopper from an early morning lift-off in Carrollton, Texas. With the recent fire and the flash floods, Fields decided to fold, cancel the project citing bad juju and the loss of money he was no longer willing to lose.

Grits awoke in a sweat the night before after dreaming all his teeth fell out. That did it for him. An omen he interpreted as predicting the death of his money was worse than sleeping in a hole full of rabid prairie dogs. The pipeline must go down the tubes.

Maybe he'd invest in a football team to challenge the Cowboys. Maybe he'd brew craft beer. Maybe he'd bring back some cotton fields worked by white pure-blooded, homogeneous, native born West Texas crackers who, unlike modern-day black folks, still didn't know they had rights.

Either way, Grits committed to wrapping up the project. The environmentalists who picketed his office and hit his wife, Della, in the face with a cream pie that day after church might give him an award.

On the way to the pipeline, Stiletto swung by the old Boy Scout camp where his deputy sheriff dad molested boys and served as master in the 50s. Stiletto regularly parked there and spied on the uppity women who lived in a commune. Using high-powered German binoculars to see if he could catch one of them topless stepping in or out of the hot tub they had set up near the kitchen door, Stiletto settled in.

Not knowing the women tracked him on security video from the time he turned off the road until he parked in the same hidden spot in the brush, the deputy never failed to unzip and pull at himself, sometimes grunting shrilly and throwing the smut magazine out the marked squad car window while in the throes of self-induced passion. The Mother Earth Patrol had Stiletto's sexual gyrations on video, too, and expected to post their catch on the sheriff's association Facebook page one day soon.

This time, instead of whipping out his usual weapon of choice, Stiletto whipped out his phone and shot several pictures of the psychedelic VW bus parked by Tripper's netted jeep. A vintage lowrider Lincoln also seemed as out of place at the camp as Stiletto's presence at a convention of capable law enforcement officers.

As he watched the camp, Branch watched him. Perched high in a redwood growing beside the car, she expertly and quietly rappelled to a lower branch. Dropping again, she considered landing on the roof but thought better of such brash action. As Branch pondered her next move, she saw Tripper backing out of the main house, holding the head end of a body tightly secured in a sturdy antique straitjacket. Other women held the torso from the bottom on both sides. Jesús brought up the rear, carrying the legs. The team uncovered Tripper's Jeep, gently placed Wally in the back and watched as Tripper and Jesús drove away.

"Where will they take him?" Rose asked.

"Somewhere safe," Wallace said.

"Being held prisoner is no fun," Rose said. "By the way, where'd they get the straitjacket?"

"Mother Jones used to be a nurse in an old school mental hospital. The jacket is a memento from her youth," Wallace said.

Silently rubbing his eyes and turning away so Rose wouldn't see him cry, he walked back inside as everyone followed.

Like a hungry black widow spider descending from her lair after spotting an unsuspecting snack, Branch pounced.

THE BUDDHA'S EYEBALL

SWIRLS of Japanese pine incense smoke curled to the roof, drifting past sunlight that broke through cracks in the cave. Volcanic matter created the cave 20,000 years ago when molten lava flowed through the deep narrow grotto. Now, ancient bat guano packed the walls, undisturbed in the flickering candlelight.

Om studied the gray shadows with the eye of the artist he was. Bat shit didn't bother him or the monks who lived and practiced Zen in several chambers that descended from an above-ground entrance hidden by a boulder and ran deep underground.

Fishing, hunting and gathering shaped secluded days. Surviving on nature, the small group of male and female monastics rarely ventured into civilization. Self-sufficient, all graduates of good colleges and universities, the group included a political scientist, a professional bagpipe player, an international jungle survival school instructor, a Grand Canyon wilderness guide and one former tobacco factory union worker from North Carolina who straddled the time and space between past and present lives.

Healthy, well-trained and devoted to studying the self, these Buddhist monks knew they would not live forever. That knowledge sculpted their attitude toward a simple life in the here-and-now. Everything is connected, everything is impermanent, and everything changes.

Live now because everything dies.

Protective of their roshi and territory, the monks practiced peace of mind. Like Yamabushi mountain warriors of eighth and ninth century Japan, they lived off the land and engaged the spiritual changes in their personal universe moment-by-moment. Strict disciplinarians, this crowd was still weird, even by hippy-dippy California standards.

Ears that looked like a bat's wings framed Om's head. A long-ago broken nose leaned left in the middle of his face. Large white teeth showed when he laughed or cried out in pain. A deep blue scar ran from the corner of his left eye down his cheek to his chin, the result of a straight razor that years ago could have taken off his head had he not moved as quickly as he did when a mad monk tried to cut his throat. Not everything about Buddhism was peace and love. Enlightened Buddhists could be devils, too.

Loading string bags and homemade crates onto the cart he fashioned from drift wood and tree branches, Om looked forward to the walk into the village for supplies. Seven miles each way gave him enough time to enjoy the mountain air, the exercise and the rare contact with civilians in town. Today he would enjoy meeting the woman he knew from the prison. Tripper contacted him through his trusted connection in the village who had done time with her in prison.

Trouble, Tripper said.

Help.

Working in the prison teaching meditation for a few weeks a few years ago helped Om learn more about injustice. He wanted to help the female inmates gain strength to release their minds, free their unstable selves, and vanquish their egos. A few weeks' instruction had given them the basics to unshackle their chains even behind bars.

The woman who called herself Tripper took her studies the most seriously—so much so that he offered to guide her when guards finally opened the front gate for her, but only if she ever took zazen seriously enough to practice full-time. Until now she never called.

Like Bodhidharma who taught the first Shaolin fighting monks, Om taught his students to look at life through the Buddha's eyeball. Big, wide-open, glaring, unblinking and focused attention to detail always paid off. Insight disappears at death, but no sooner. In life, the Buddha's eyeball never closes.

"Don't tell me. That's him," Jesús said.

Tripper clapped her hands.

"Om hasn't changed a bit."

Wally slept comfortably, snug as a bug in a rug.

Sandals made from tree bark and vines slapped against the side of the road, raising dust as the monk drew nearer. A long thin coat made from goat hide, closed with buttons carved from the creature's black hooves, fell to his ankles. Om wore a cone-shaped hat made from a thicker vine. The monk looked fit and in fighting shape.

"Tripper," he said.

"Om."

Jesús extended his hand.

"Jesús Zarate."

"Even asleep, the man wearing the straitjacket in your Jeep is giving off some heavy vibes," Om said.

"Where can we talk?" Tripper asked.

"Let me grab a few items, some wine and a couple of six packs, and you can give me a ride back to the dirt road. You have society's steel cage out of your system yet?"

"I do," she said.

"Looks like we have a lot to talk about," Om said.

"Will you help us? " Tripper asked.

"I will," he said. "As long as you're willing to see through the Buddha's eyeball."

WHITE HOT

STILETTO'S eyes closed as he dozed.

Rappelling silently to the ground, Branch landed without a sound and crab crawled on her back under Stiletto's police car. Carefully wiring the dynamite she slid from her backpack to the undercarriage, she attached the detonators and fuses. Five minutes passed. Ten minutes passed.

Off the pig.

Branch stood, unfolding like a young sapling. Sensing a presence, Stiletto gasped. As her head came to eye level, he went for his gun, but his unbuckled belt got in the way and the holster and gun fell to the floor by the gas pedal.

"What's your sign?" Branch said through the open window. "Don't tell me. Let me guess. Sagittarius? Gemini? Pisces?"

"Aquarium," Stiletto whispered.

To complement her syrupy tone loaded with the promise of loose love, she licked her lips the way she imagined hookers would do. Reaching for Stiletto's head, she curled a strand of Stiletto's hair around her finger and fondled his ear lobe.

Stiletto whimpered like an old dog catching a whiff of a Spam sandwich.

"What do you want?" he asked.

"I want you to protect and serve me," she said.

Fumbling with his pants, Stiletto threw aside his porn magazines and adjusted his boner. Almost falling out of the driver's side, Stiletto raced around the rear of the car to open the back door.

Pushing Branch in first, he pulled the door closed behind him.

Settling in comfortably, Stiletto took a deep breath and leaned back. When he exhaled, a thin wisp of smoke streamed from his nostrils. Looking confused, he reached for Branch, who smelled something burning. Stiletto's eyebrows started smoking. His nose hairs sizzled. Miniature flames crept up the base of his skull, sparking in his tangle of dyed black hair before stopping at his bald spot on the top of his head. Next, the hair on his hands caught fire.

"I'm burning," he whined. "I'm burning."

Even the coolest people in Northern California rarely, if ever, encounter bona fide spontaneous internal human combustion. Branch never heard of this strange phenomenon. Stiletto never knew what lit him.

Down in Mexico, in a Sinaloa sitting room, two black candles burned as bright beacons of justice for the oppressed, the vulnerable and the dispossessed. Zita swayed from side to side in a trance that brought to her the fragrance of dragon fruit flowers as she burned rat hair in a clay bowl.

Branch knew she damn well better get out of the car, but Stiletto had secured the suspect proof locks and she found no escape after the cop passed out from his fear of fire. Starting to burn faster, his ass, like thick, white lard in a pan, set the seat ablaze, charring the back seat foam rubber and igniting the dynamite fuses.

Pounding on the windows, Branch bellowed to no avail.

The car blew.

A small funeral complete with departmental honors would commence in a few days.

No tribute was forthcoming for Charlie Manson's granddaughter.

A week later all that remained of Branch's legacy was a modest bundle of White Sage and a humble offering of showstopper pink western redbud bush, planted with affection in the dirt by grieving women who still counted her as a sister.

ENTER THE DEADEYE

CROUCHING before the mirror in his Elk motel room, Deadeye practiced personalized secret martial arts training—ancient Kung Fu moves kept under cover by a long line of teachers of "the realm," according to Master Chow, whom Deadeye met when Chow was working at the noodle shop washing dishes and Deadeye came in for the all-you-can-slurp special.

Chow, goofing on this monotonous macho hick by initiating him into the fabricated Chop Suey School of Martial Disorder and Death, told Deadeye he must practice one technique and one technique only. The deadly move, designed specifically for Deadeye at a price based on Chow's aptitude for diagnosing martial prowess, could render an opponent helpless and send even a master into the depth of shock after just one application.

Drawn from ancient Mo Goo teachings, the master called Deadeye's personal secret technique "Foo You," which, in the dialect of Chow's imaginary warriors, means "The Final Finger." Inflicting the final finger defense on an attacker would end even the most fearsome confrontation. A devastating single finger fracture could reduce the strongest assailant to tears before fainting from pain. The world's toughest thugs are not used to having their digits snapped in front of them, Master Chow said.

To reach such lethal level of expertise, however, the student must practice.

Save all the bones from your country-fried chicken wing dinners, Chow said. Dry the skeletal parts. Keep them in a sack. Carry them over your shoulder like Hotei, the laughing Buddha. Break 50 bones each day. Imagine fingers closing around your throat. Splinter them. Imagine a bail jumper pointing his finger in your chest. Snap it. Practice the secret sauce style not of Wing Chun, but of Chicken Wing Chun.

Deadeye practiced breaking chicken bones until his fingerprints hurt.

Until now, all Deadeye was good for in a fight was jumping on an opponent's back, holding on for dear life, and sinking his teeth into the shoulder meat. Now, though, he was a certified black belt, registered with Master Chow and the Moo Goo Society. With a red tattoo he gave himself on the inside of his right forearm that said "Foo Yoo" and a trail of demolished chicken bones as his legacy, Deadeye checked out of the motel and went to meet the mission head on.

Lucky for him his degenerate street source tipped him to Animal's targets after Animal got chopped up in Shell Beach. Lucky big mouth Rose and Wallace busted off about the lodge where they were headed. Lucky Deadeye trained daily to take on these refugees who flew the coop. Nothing would stand in the way of him and a well-deserved payday—a rare enough occurrence as it was.

By the time Deadeye reached Navarro (population 142 give or take a dozen either way) he started noticing a variety of vehicles passing him or heading in the same direction. All bore black flags or pieces of black cloth on their antennas. One well-used Bronco carried a message in white paint on the rear window that began to explain the flags.

"Rest in peace Weed Eaters."

Deadeye heard about the local massacre on the radio—a team of paramilitary pot growers slaughtered in a firefight with unknown assailants. Killers on the loose and on the run resulted in an all-points bulletin for what seemed to be rival marijuana farmers who would stone you to death with real stones if you messed with their product or their stash.

Despite the Weed Eaters' reputation for homegrown ignorance and wanton violence, rare but not unheard of in Northern California, genuine stoners did their best to stick together. That's why reefer heads far and wide planned as big a send-off as they could throw for the boys, a funeral to rival anything Deadheads provided for Jerry Garcia or enjoyed by any other West Coast drug pioneer, including Timothy Leary. Pot paeans were in order, a good time would be had by all, and Deadeye was always looking for a party. Besides, Stiletto wasn't answering his phone.

Spotting what looked like an orgy in a wild flower field of fire-cracker lilies, blue-eyed grass and mule ears, Deadeye pulled over and undid his ponytail. Stringy reddish-blond hair cascaded below his shoulders. Always as cool as the next guy in Deadeye's mind, he grabbed his bota bag wineskin loaded with chardonnay and made his way into the crowd.

Holding the wineskin about an inch from his nose, he tilted the spout so wine would pour into his mouth. Raising the skin, he felt like an Athenian shepherd on a heavenly hillside, a Dionysian example of drunken impishness, ecstatic in his passionate lack of reason and shame. Wine dribbled down his chin soaking his black T-shirt and matching leather vest. Unhinged as he was, Deadeye started to dance playfully to the sound of the drum circle that hammered out a rhythm of debauchery into his brain, moving across the field with the delicate ease of a Greek satyr high on crack and morning glory seeds.

Collapsing out of breath, he fell on a soft carpet of leaves. Stretched out and tired from the long drive the day before, 20 minutes of secret Kung Fu practice and the two Seconals he ate for lunch that slowed the activity of his cortex, Deadeye quickly lost consciousness. Other celebrants saw his guns exposed and decided to leave him alone until he awoke. Maybe then they could reason with this barbarian who apparently shared some unknown common purpose, saw the light, and came to dance, get high and, hopefully, give up his guns and share the love.

Deadeye slept too soundly for his own good.

Feeling sorry for this nomad, a woman adorned in a California Republic bear flag tank top in red, green and black Rasta colors covered him in marijuana leaves so he'd stay warm. As the night wore on, more and more mourners danced around the growing carpet of pot leaves, buds and flowers into which Deadeye collapsed, adding their own mounting contribution to a historic community project on the exact spot where Deadeye had collapsed.

But when the dope blanket got so thick they could no longer see him, these merry rascals forgot all about him.

Overcome with emotion, on this day our intrepid band of doobie brothers and sisters would go down in history as creators of the world's biggest joint, rolled in honor of the Weed Eaters and their demise. By midnight Deadeye was part of history. Totally and communally rolled in pot, he became one with the big dub that extended 12 feet long and was about as wide as a loosely wound living room carpet. Two dozen people on their knees, so wrecked they didn't notice the bump that was Deadeye, expertly rolled that super joint, encasing the bombed bounty hunter in a leafy tomb to be lit as a grand finale at the Weed Eater funeral.

Project leaders had no idea how to actually smoke their giant joint. They just knew they had become crackerjack space cowboys who produced a hemp paper roll unlike any other in the universe, a landmark project that by 4 a.m. was complete—ends twisted and everything, entombing Deadeye who had stopped breathing by hours earlier, asphyxiated like fucking totally.

The next morning, when the whammy bammy bearers loaded their masterpiece on the truck, somebody noticed a flash of black denim. Deadeye's Levis gave him away and created such a major bummer panic when Weed Eater wannabees pulled his remains free from the giant joint that a whole third of the wrecked crowd passed on the services and got busy ingesting any and every substance they could find.

One extremist actually proposed smoking Deadeye.

"How the fuck would you even do that, man?"

"In a really big bong?"

As a gesture of respect in Deadeye's honor, organizers just dug another hole by the Weed Eaters' opening in the earth and dumped the clod into the chasm.

"Rest in peace, bro," said a nude man in a top hat with his public hair painted red, white and blue.

RAID

WHEN the SWAT team hit the lodge door, wood splinters flew and hinges tore from their bindings. Menacing police dogs strained at their leashes, and cops bellowing orders with laser sights on automatic weapons pushed into each other in their hurry to capture the serial killers who were ruining wine country tourism by leaving a long blood trail up the coast—fruitcakes who must be stopped at all cost.

Hysteria aside, the women of the house merely looked up from their knitting and crocheting like the cops had just interrupted a senior citizen crumpet social.

"May we help you?" Becky asked.

"Don't you move," the tactical sergeant fumed.

"Might I at least put down my knitting needle?" Becky asked.

"Slowly," said the sergeant in charge.

Mother Jones glared and cleared her throat.

"I assume you gentlemen, and I use that word loosely, have a warrant," she said.

They didn't.

"Based on life and death confidential information we just received, we decided to stop a criminal conspiracy in motion," the sergeant said.

"We're making pussy hats," Becky said.

"Watch your mouth, ma'am," a SWAT captain said.

"Don't call me ma'am, officer," Becky said. "I'm not the fucking Queen Mother and you're not Joe Friday."

The cops originally showed for the reported explosion called in by a LGBTQ bird watching group that turned into what police decided was a full-blown murder/suicide—and they weren't sure who murdered who—rather than the suspected assassination of a law enforcement official by a radical female jihadist. Not much evidence survived to assemble a case. The forensics team had enough trouble assembling pieces of Branch and Stiletto to bag, tag and ship to the coroner's office.

Police also botched a chance to make some real headway with the wine trail killings. After playing a hunch when they earlier heard the first chopper blades in the distance, Rose and Wallace slipped out the back door and headed deep into the trees. Equipped with rucksacks, food, water and other supplies to last them a comfortable week underground, they hiked back to the pit to hide out. Going in clean and sober this time made the flashbacks more than bearable. Spending time snuggling would be downright enjoyable.

"We already called the TV station," Mother Jones said as a police tow truck hooked up Wally's VW van. "A crew is on the way."

Wallace and Jesús had the forethought to bury the bike and the low-rider in a thicket about a mile from the cabin.

"Would you boys like some brownies?" Mother Jones asked. "We have hash and hashless."

"That would be nice," said one of the strike force troopers. "Hash, please."

"Goddammit, officer," the sergeant said.

"We're videoing this drama, by the way," said Mother Jones. "Your bullying is out of line. Your aggression is unacceptable. Your trying to cover up potential drug use by one of your fly SWATTERs is atrocious. We are a civic group. I am a golden ager. You are the oppressive thugs of the state. You should know that we expect to start weeping openly with our hands up begging for mercy on our knees when the reporters show up."

"So there's nobody here we need to talk to," the sergeant said.

"Nobody but us girls," Mother Jones said.

"Abort, abort," the SWAT captain shouted into his radio. "Mission aborted."

Then they were gone. A tense silence filled the air for about 15 seconds. The sound of hovering chopper blades over the cabin disappeared as did a handful of hash brownies.

"Abort, abort," Becky said. "At least they're pro-choice."

Breaking out the sherry and what was left of the brownies, the Mother Earth Patrol settled in for the night. Mother Jones asked if anybody was interested in her recipe for homemade napalm.

Everyone was.

Nobody noticed the coyote looking in the window.

ESCAPE

WITH his hands folded across his chest, Wally stayed calm and focused. Nurse Mother Jones had firmly fastened five brown leather straps at the back of the straitjacket. Long loose arms of the straitjacket extended beyond Wally's fingertips and attached at the back as well.

Leaning back against the monastery's cave wall, Wally knew he had to break out.

Standing to full height and bending at the waist, skinny Wally took a deep breath and exhaled, making sure to make his upper body muscles as small as possible. Shaking back and forth, left and right, to get some space between his body and the thick white canvas jacket, within seconds Wally had enough room to extend his strong left arm over his head followed by his weaker lower arm. Undoing the sleeve buckle with his teeth, he reached around his back and undid the top strap. Bending again, he shook and shook and eventually worked the jacket over his head, backing out of the garment and throwing it on the floor in one minute and 45 seconds.

Thankful he had regularly practiced this useless trick when he was in his early 20s and infatuated with magic, Wally felt energized and full of purpose. As his own worst enemy, Wally knew the time had come to fight back.

"Nice job, Houdini," Syrah spit. "At least you didn't have to pull that stunt hanging upside down from a crane."

"Syrah, stop," Wally said.

"Stop, shit," she said.

"No, I mean it," he said. "I control you."

Syrah wailed.

"If you controlled me we wouldn't be in this mess," she said. "We wouldn't be partners in crime and time."

"You want out as much as I do," Wally said.

Moving slowly, he spotted two monks in black robes raking sand circles in a garden where gray stones rose like the tips of broken samurai swords growing from the earth. So intent in their focus, they didn't see him as he slid into the tree line and blended with the foliage. Wally began to jog, breathing steadily, feeling power build in his legs. Pumping his arms lightly, he stretched to full height as he ran. Smelling the air, the dank moss underfoot energized him even more.

Freedom lives here, Wally thought.

"Unchain your mind, Syrah," he said. "We're finally on our way."

No one would save him now. No one would help him. He could only help himself. Only he could free his mind and hers. Only he could live the legacy his sainted mother left him. Honor, respect, love—what she taught—now embodied Wally.

But he was sick, sick, sick, too far gone to get better.

"You're tiring me out," Syrah said. "Let's stop for a glass of wine. You like chardonnay, Wally?"

"Shhhh," Wally said. "Be at peace."

Sprinting to a sacred place he first saw as the Jeep made the turn toward the monastery, Wally knew he was meant to "be here now" as a prophet once said, to relinquish all suffering for those who also suffer, those who needed his example. Few people ever tried to stop him as he squandered his life. Now he would be there for them—forgo his own life and future and vow to save all sentient beings. His mother would be thrilled that Wally looked at life through the Buddha's eyeball, just like the big boss monk they picked up in the Jeep told Tripper and Jesús they must do.

Wondering if he had been enlightened, Wally decided he had.

At that he stopped running.

Facing a barrier he immediately christened "Rock Buddha," he saw no eyes, no ears, no nose or mouth. Three large smooth boulders sat one on top of the other. Without a face, this Buddha offered no

clue to emotion, resemblance or identity. Wally remembered reading about how mountain monks who lived in seclusion sometimes
stacked three rocks on top of each other as Buddha reminders, as
if the ground rock served as the base, the middle rock functioned
as the body, and the top rock acted as the head. Like those faceless
Buddhas, directionless, motionless satori would absorb him.

Wally was the Buddha.

The Buddha was Wally.

Wally Buddha lived.

Now Buddha Wally must die.

Kill the Buddha.

Kill Wally.

Reciting the traditional Evening Gatha he had memorized as a
teenager when he first became interested in Zen Buddhism, Wally
mindfully pronounced each word.

"Let me respectfully remind you. Life and death are of supreme
importance. Time swiftly passes by and opportunity is lost. Each of
us should strive to awaken... awaken. Take heed. Do not squander
your life."

"Please don't, Wally," Syrah said. "I love you."

"It's too late for us," Wally said. "I love you, too, Syrah."

Distancing himself from Syrah's command, Wally struggled
to tune her out.

"You got your corkscrew, Wally? Bet those monks are drinking
chardonnay right now and laughing at you," she said.

"Yes, I have my corkscrew, Syrah."

"Tripper and Jesús look like chardonnay drinkers to me."

"They're partial to pinot, Syrah."

"Don't you do this, Wally."

As Wally moved closer to Rock Buddha, a 1600 watt, 45-pound,
portable red Honda inverter gasoline-powered generator seemed to
appear out of nowhere. So did the full gas can that leaned against a
tree, resting on a throw rug decorated with a stitched picture of a
wide-antlered buck, a doe and her fawn.

"Yeah, these monks sure are roughing it, Wally," Syrah said. "Making lattes and watching the Raiders' games with their own gas generator."

Wally ignored the indefatigable curse that had turned his life into a fiendish sham.

Approaching with deference, seeing life and death come together, he slowly turned his back on Rock Buddha. Flaming images blinked off and on in his mind. A sad story about a bold hero his mother told him about a long time ago materialized among the many mental memes he carried for better or for worse. The mental picture spoke of pure sacrifice, highlighting an offering provided by a solitary man, a Buddhist monk in Vietnam where corruption, violence and sadness controlled the lives of countless people.

In the spirit of that great holy man, gently dropping to his left knee and then his right, Wally kneeled with his knees together and his back straight, sitting with his heels touching his buttocks, assuming the classic traditional seiza sitting position of Japan. Placing his hands palm down on his thighs, Wally let himself go.

"I mean it," Syrah said. "You can't do this."

Wally chose not to respond.

Gentle wind caressed his cheeks. The tip of his nose itched. A throbbing pain in his left ankle made him want to adjust but he stayed still. So alive and knowing it, Wally slowed his breathing, trying to savor each instant of each moment. Life's essence belonged to him.

"You're going to do it, aren't you?" Syrah asked. "You're really going to do it."

Wally listened to high-pitched notes of a birdsong and said nothing.

Lowering his eyes, he saw a glint of gold. Slowly reaching, he plucked a small chunk of iron pyrite, fool's gold, from the dirt. Rubbing the pyramid-shaped mineral with his fingers, Wally felt confident, sensing an unfamiliar urge to act and not react. Sunshine flashed in the golden dazzle of the rock. Power from the earth seemed to connect with the sun. Wally was on his way to the cosmos.

Leaning left, Wally opened and closed his hand on the gas can handle. Pulling the full container close, he watched the brimming liquid shift below the small opening at the top of the can. Smelling pungent fumes, Wally raised the gas can to shoulder height and began to pour. The first cold splash on his shoulder stung. Closing his eyes, he raised his arm, tilting the metal spout toward his face, pouring fresh gasoline over his head. Running down his shoulders, back and chest, the liquid burned, stinging his eyes as he tasted his final fill-up.

Squeezing the yellowish mineral in the palm of his hand, Wally dug into the pocket of his jeans, connecting with the cold steel of the corkscrew. Pulling the instrument from his pocket, he lightly scratched the metal point against the rock. Scratching again against the fool's gold, this time harder, he felt foolhardy and knew the time to go for broke had finally arrived. Grasping the corkscrew tighter, he ripped the sharp point across the surface of the rock, harshly scraping the steel point against the pyrite.

One small spark was all it took.

In his ears Wally heard a dull echo that sounded like an aged basement furnace flutter to life on a cold day. The first flame scorched Wally's waist, joining another rush of flame that clutched Wally's chest. Fire fingers drew upward, choking air from Wally's nostrils, burning into his eye sockets, turning his eyebrows and lips black. Despite the torturous eruption of singed flesh across Wally's face, a beatific relaxation caressed dying muscles that no longer could protect bone that no longer could protect the brain that fought to live and pulse with emotion and sensation.

Lowering his gaze and covering his right upturned palm with the top of his left hand, Wally touched the tips of his thumbs together in the sign of a mudra that gathered and guided energy flow to his brain.

Wally willed his mind to stop.

Syrah went silent.

A bonfire now, Wally sat in perfect stillness. Consumed by his personal inferno, Wally felt the end become the beginning. Blood flow to and from his heart slowed, producing another dynamic plane of energy that coursed through his body, enveloping universal forces that make us what we are and what we are not.

Wally whispered his last words.

"One more step," he said.

Taking a final breath, Wally died inside and out. No bongos beat a frantic rhythm. No surf guitar electrified his soul. In the distance, a monk struck a temple bell with a stick, producing one long gong that reverberated and filled the still cavern of Wally's emptiness. Dignified and upright until the smoke settled, gravity gently nudged him onto his side as his blood bubbled and simmered. Wally went away forever, his crisp skin bag smoking like a bacon breakfast fire that careless campers forgot to extinguish before turning their backs on a cold mountain and hiking deeper into the mystery of their own carefree lives.

RETREAT

"THIS really is the pits, Wallace," Rose said.

Playfully punching her on the arm, Wallace laughed and covered up as she unleashed her own barrage of body blow love taps that pushed him back against the dirt wall of the pit that once held them captive.

Now they called the shots—safe, isolated and together again.

Before going into hiding, they built a plywood cover, pasting thick moss, grass and leaves to the lid before Rose climbed down the ladder and Wallace closed the cover over them. The roof would hold even if a search party was standing right on top of them.

A soft blow-up mattress, two battery-operated military grade "Tac" lights, a folding camper's table and chairs, and meals ready to eat that produced no cooking aroma made for a comfy little room in which they planned to spend two days and two nights, longer if need be. The search party would leave by then, figuring they got away. With Wallace's background as a combat recon scout, they could easily find their way to the monastery. A map, military compass and other survival aides made outrunning the cops almost embarrassing and easier than ever.

Maybe God existed, Wallace thought, trying to figure out the coincidence of Tripper's guru and the grave of his dead buddy from the war being within easy driving distance of each other. Nah, he thought, a real God just wouldn't put good people through this shit. Thinking back to the last conversation he had with his father, he remembered Wally telling him there is no beginning and no end.

Wallace liked that.

So did Wally.

"I almost wish we had champagne," Rose said.

Before Wallace could chastise her, she laughed and said, "I'm just busting you."

"You think we're strong enough to joke about that?" he asked.

"I do," she said.

"Withdrawal was bad."

"Other factors complicated our detox," she said.

"But we're clean."

"We are."

Rose opened a bottle of water, took a long swig, and handed the plastic bottle to Wallace.

"We'll have to pee in front of each other," he said.

"Just close your eyes and imagine it's raining," she said.

Reaching into his pack, Wallace produced disposal waste bags equipped with chemical odor removers they could use and bury in the corner of the pit.

"My hero," Rose said. "You thought of everything."

"No," he said. "The Mother Earth Patrol thought of everything. They were equipped for a nuclear attack. I sure could have used their backup in Afghanistan. Maybe Skeeter would still be alive."

"Maybe we can make it, Wallace," Rose said.

"When we get to the monastery, let's settle in until we decide what to do," Wallace said. "Tripper says Om is a good, courageous man who will help us and my dad."

"You think Wally will be all right."

"I do, Rose," Wallace said. "Yes, I do."

"You think we can stay at the monastery for good?" Rose asked.

"Live in a cave forever?"

"Yeah," she said.

"That's deep."

Wallace and Rose lovingly punched each other like a couple of young monkeys playing in the trees.

EMBERS

DRAPING thick canvas over Wally's smoldering charred remains, the monks gently extinguished flickering flames that still flared around his corpse. Tucking the tarp under his body, the men and women lifted, gently carrying him to Tripper's truck.

"Wally wanted to help." Jesús said.

"Wally didn't want to hurt anybody," Tripper said.

"More sacrificial lamb than shepherd," Om said. "We will conduct a simple ceremony. We will keep his remains in an urn and his spirit in our hearts."

"What will you tell the police?" Jesús asked.

"The truth," Om said. "That's the whole point, right?"

"Tell them we were here," Tripper said.

"I will," Om said.

"Tell them our whole story, everything we told you," Jesús said. "I will."

"Crazy as it sounds, it's all true," Jesús said.

"Life is always all true," Om said. "Even the lies."

"Will you drive us back to Tripper's camp to pick up my car?" Jesús said.

"No need for two vehicles," Tripper said. "You want my Jeep, Om?"

"You sure?"

"I'm not sure of anything at this point."

"Then where you headed?" Om said.

"We're going to Mexico," Jesús said. "My mother is waiting."

"What about you?" Tripper asked Om.

"I write poems on fallen leaves and drop them into mountain streams. I write poems on dog biscuits and leave them along the trail so the coyotes can eat. I turn over rocks and write poems on the bottoms before turning them back and replacing them on the ground."

"That's pretty far out, Om," Tripper said.

"Actually, it's pretty far in," he said. "Pretty far into the brightest cavern of my mind."

"A great warrior once said, 'Fight ten thousand like one and one like ten thousand,'" Jesús said.

"Then send them on their way," Om said.

"Wallace and Rose will be here in a few days," Tripper said. "What will you tell them?"

"The truth, right?" Jesús said.

"They'll be all right," Om said. "We'll all be all right. Truth makes everything right."

Tripper tossed the keys to Om, who caught them in one smooth motion, turned and walked to the Jeep. Starting the engine, he gunned the gas pedal before stepping on the clutch and grinding the transmission into gear. Jesús and Tripper climbed in. Pulling away, they glanced at Rock Buddha.

The Buddha's eyeball saw nothing.

The Buddha's eyeball saw everything.

Nothing special means everything special.

THE GIFT

Broken Pacifico beer bottles littered gutters near the Jesús Malverde shrine in Culiacan, Mexico. Squealing children set off fireworks in a densely populated neighborhood of bright tiny houses and dull melancholy shacks. Greasy tortilla smells filled the afternoon air. A cat bawled in heat.

Kneeling before a ceramic bust of the narco-saint, a large man wearing an immaculate white cowboy hat said his prayers to the angel of the poor. The man himself was once poor. Now he controlled Sinaloa's drug trade, scaring even the cartel's top hit men. Arturo's smile meant death. That smile signaled when another body would fall and another man would die. Arturo often boasted he had never killed a woman, a child or a dog—at least not yet. If worse came to worst, he said he would kill men, women and children all at the same time.

Arturo worked out every day pumping iron weights, boxing with his young bodyguards, running in the early morning—all to keep the fat from collecting around his midsection like the soft underbelly of a prize young bull at the country cattle fair. But nothing could save Arturo from the contract a rival cartel put out on him that morning. Nothing could keep Arturo from his date with death—nothing except the power his sister, Zita, wielded in her mind. But she was not so lovingly inclined.

"When will the hitmen come, Zita?"

"Soon."

"Where will I hide?"

"In your fantasies."

Arturo squinted.

"You never change," he said. "Talking in charades suits you."

The narcotraffickers claimed to respect Jesus Malverde. But Arturo's line of work dishonored the simple roots of innocence and love that drove Malverde to his humanitarian mission and made Zita a good witch.

"I only tell you what I see," Zita said. I cannot change the life forces that light up your fate. I only pray that goodness acts as your shield."

"I am not a good man."

"You will change," she said. "When you die."

"Have you heard from your son, Jesús?"

"He will arrive in a week to take a newspaper columnist job here in Culiacan."

"He is ready for the challenges of this city?"

"This is his blood home. His biggest test is over," Zita said. "After all these years, he has finally faced himself."

"Most men never do," Arturo said.

"Jesús will now claim his family surname, his real name," Zita said. "Embody the reincarnation of his great-grandfather, Jesús Malverde, proclaim Malverde's resurrection, declare Malverde's rebirth."

"Jesús Malverde has risen," Arturo said.

"Sí," Zita said. "Our sweet saint tells me he is proud his DNA runs in my son's veins. My Jesús will help the poor. Jesús will right the wrongs. Jesús will stand against the evil cartels. Men like you, Arturo."

Arturo stood in shame.

Outside on a hard, dusty street, a rawboned teenage accordion player played a narcorrido ballad, singing an off-key tribute to the great Mexican peasant king of the people.

"Jesús Malverde is a man just like me—a man of great power and rich history. Our time will soon come because of his fame. Our bright destiny a new savior will claim."

High above the rooftops a mighty prairie falcon flashed its talons and circled high in the sky above Culiacan, a glint of sunbeam flashing from a small silver peace symbol hanging from its neck on a silver chain.

Two thousand miles north, one very matter-of-fact scorpion rode with great poise on the back seat of a flat black 1963 Lincoln Continental low-rider, speeding south through seemingly endless chardonnay vineyards on sundrenched California blacktop.

In the front seat two happy newlyweds raced toward the rest of their lives in savage Mexican bandit country, passing an open bottle of blood red syrah between them.

Viva libertad.

Viva justicia.

Viva Jesús Malverde.

The End

email steve@bloodredsyrah.com

www.bloodredsyrah.com

Made in the USA
Monee, IL
18 October 2024

67465068R00148